Comfort Me

Other Books by Debbie Viguié

Comfort Me

Psalm 23 Mysteries

By Debbie Viguié

Published by Big Pink Bow

Comfort Me

ISBN-13: 978-0-9906971-5-2

Published by Big Pink Bow

www.bigpinkbow.com

Dedicated to Diane Woodall - without your help I would have gone crazy this past year.

Thank you to everyone who helped make this book a reality, particularly Barbara Reynolds, Rick Reynolds, Calliope Collacott, and Chrissy Current. I also need to thank all the fans who have waited so patiently for this book.

1

Cindy Preston dreaded Tuesdays now that they had become the new Mondays. It had been a month since she quit her job at the church. She had immediately signed up with a temp agency and she kept getting four-day assignments, always starting on a Tuesday because somehow people didn't realize they were going to need a temporary administrative assistant until Monday mid-morning. At that point they'd call the staffing agency which would then call her. For someone who had always avoided uncertainty and change the process had been agonizing.

It was Tuesday and she had another slip of paper in her hand with another new address on it. This assignment would be different, though. Supposedly the company was going to need her services for four to six weeks while they conducted interviews for a permanent administrative assistant.

She arrived at the building. A chain link fence surrounded the entire property. *Friendly place*, she thought with a grimace. The gate was open and she pulled slowly up to the guard station.

The guard, a tall thin man with a shock of red hair, scowled at her. "Can I help you, Miss?"

"Yes, I'm Cindy Preston, the new temp. Mr. Cartwright is expecting me," she said.

"Let me see your driver's license," he said, scowl still firmly in place.

Cindy fished it out of her purse, wishing that there wasn't a cold little knot of dread settling in her stomach. She was working overtime trying not to feel negative about the place.

He handed it back to her. "Park in the back row," he said pointing to the section of cars farthest from the building. "Take the elevator to the fifth floor."

"Thank you," she started to say, but he'd already turned away, effectively dismissing her.

Cindy eased her car forward and then made her way to the parking section he'd indicated. She got the very last slot in the row which had her in the far corner by the chain link fences. She was also the farthest away from the building she could possibly be.

"It's going to be fine," she told herself as she turned off the ignition.

She pulled her deck of cards out of her purse and then got out of the car. She locked it, shouldered her purse, and then began cutting the cards one-handed, her hand held at waist-level while she walked toward the building.

By the looks of it, there were probably only a total of five or six floors in the building. What it lacked in height, though, it more than made up for in sprawling bulk. She was walking toward a massive open door that a forklift was driving slowly out of. Several other large pieces of equipment were parked in the area closest to the building.

Above the entrance was a simple sign that read *Rayburn NextGen Solutions*. She marched toward it, eyes moving around the parking lot as she went, trying to get a feel for the place and the people and equipment that might be nearby.

Cindy realized that as her stomach tightened up more she was shuffling the cards faster and faster. Change was hard. She'd gotten used to having a little change in her life over the last few years, but this felt like a lot. It was hard not knowing where she was going to work or what was going to be expected of her once she got there. So far there was no luck finding a permanent job. It was probably just as well. She couldn't imagine working for any of the places that she'd temped for. Her stress levels were high which was why she'd been using the cards a lot more lately to try and calm herself down. It was a habit she'd thought herself nearly broken of until the job crisis. There were worse habits, that was for sure. At least hers wasn't dangerous or rude or messy.

She made it to the front of the building and peered anxiously into the building's darkened maw. She took a timid step forward, half-expecting to see another forklift to come barreling toward her.

There was a lot of noise, shouting, the sounds of equipment moving, but nothing seemed to be coming at her. She took a couple more steps, her eyes slowly adjusting to the dimness after the bright light outside. There was a wall to her right that ran about ten feet before ending abruptly. An elevator door was in the middle of it. She moved quickly to the elevator and pressed the call button.

When the doors slid open she stepped forward hastily and nearly collided with a large man in an expensive grey suit who was trying to exit.

3

"Watch where you're going," he grunted as he brushed past her.

"Sorry," she said, wincing, as she stood for a moment before getting on the elevator.

She pushed the button for floor five, noting that there were six floors in the building. There was also a card reader on the keypad above the floor buttons. She wondered if she'd need a card to get to her floor.

The doors slid closed, though, and the elevator lurched sharply upward. The elevator had unadorned walls and ugly, old flooring that had probably once been cream colored. The whole thing smelled of oil and machinery. It was the type of elevator she would have expected to find in a factory and not an office building. If what she'd seen downstairs was any indication, though, this place might well be more factory than office.

The elevator came to a hard stop when it reached her floor which jolted her and put her slightly off balance. She nearly dropped her cards and her heart flew into her mouth. Playing 52 Card Pickup in there was not her idea of a good time.

She hurried off the elevator then stood, trying to figure out which way to go. To her left there were half a dozen cubicles, separated by walls that only went up about four feet. To her right it looked like there were a couple of offices. Like the elevator everything looked drab, functional, but at least it was carpeted and didn't smell of steel and grease.

She'd been told to ask for Mr. Kenneth Cartwright. She turned to the right. The rooms that could be offices had their doors closed, and there were no identifying marks on them to denote what they were or who might be behind them. She turned back the other way and approached the first cubicle.

The guy sitting in it had dark skin and close-cropped black hair. He was wearing a tie and a pale blue button-up shirt with the sleeves rolled up to his elbows. He was frowning at something he was staring at on his computer screen.

"Excuse me," she said.

He actually jumped, clearly startled and looked up at her with large eyes. He blinked several times rapidly and then asked, "Who are you?"

"My name is Cindy Preston. I'm the new temp. I was told to ask for Mr. Cartwright."

He nodded, his face relaxing into a smile. "Sorry, I didn't mean to be rude. We don't get a lot of visitors up here."

"It's fine, I'm sorry for interrupting you," she said.

He stood. "I'm Leo. Nice to meet you, Cindy," he said, extending his hand.

"Thank you. Nice to meet you, Leo."

She switched her deck of cards to her left hand so she could shake his hand. After a second he let go and sat back down. "Mr. Cartwright's office is the first one just on the other side of the elevator," he said. "He likes to keep an eye on all of us." His tone was joking but his smile didn't quite reach his eyes.

"Okay, thank you."

She turned to go. After she'd taken a couple of steps he called after her, "Good luck, Cindy."

She turned, "Why do you say that?" she asked, fear coiling inside her.

He looked at her like she was crazy, "Because you're

starting a new job. Good luck on that," he said, speaking slowly as though she were an idiot for not getting it.

Which she was. Of course that was how he'd meant it. She'd thought for a second that he was making a disparaging comment about Mr. Cartwright since he clearly didn't like the fact that the man kept his eyes on everyone so closely.

"Sorry, first day jitters," she apologized.

"You're all good," he said, turning back to his computer monitor.

Cindy was still shuffling the cards left-handed when she stopped in front of the unmarked door. She glanced back questioningly but Leo was absorbed back into his work.

She knocked on the door and waited, listening for an answer. She didn't hear one. She knocked again, much louder this time, and turned her head so her ear was close to the door. Again she couldn't hear anything. It looked like a sturdy door. It was possible that Mr. Cartwright was saying something and she couldn't hear him.

She stood there for a moment, wondering what to do. There was a clock on a nearby wall that let her know it was ten minutes after eight. She'd have to allow more time the next morning to park her car and walk to the building. She sighed, frustrated. Starting late on the first day was not a good thing.

She wished there was an administrative assistant, someone she could flag down and ask for help, but that was likely the role she was here to fill.

So, I better get around to filling it, she told herself resolutely.

She tried the doorknob and discovered that it turned freely in her hand. She pushed the door open just a little way and knocked again, "Mr. Cartwright, I'm Cindy, the temp, are you in?"

When silence continued to greet her she cautiously opened the door further and stepped inside. A terrible thought flashed through her mind and she sent up a quick prayer that she wasn't about to find him dead. A few years ago that would have seemed ridiculous to her, but now it just seemed like a good precaution.

"Hello?" she called, stepping all the way in.

The office was spacious. There was a mahogany desk at the far end of the room with an overstuffed chair behind it. There were two other chairs, one by the door and one in front of the desk. There was a bookshelf on the wall that was filled with what looked to be law books. The opposite wall held a large, framed diploma.

There were no bodies. At least, none that she could see. That was a relief. Of course, she didn't really want to step around the desk to find out.

She stood there for a few seconds, debating what to do. She had no idea where her new boss was. She contemplated taking a seat in one of the chairs and waiting for him. That might be the best choice. Otherwise she'd be standing outside for who knew how long?

She moved to the chair in front of the desk. As she did her eyes roved briefly across the desk. He kept it neat. Very, very neat. There was one small pile of papers in an inbox and stacked above it was an outbox with another similar pile of small papers. Aside from a phone, a computer monitor, and a pen there was nothing else on his desk.

That was good to know. He probably prized organization and efficiency over everything. So, she'd just have to make sure she stayed on top of things to help it all go smoothly.

"What are you doing trespassing in my office?" a rough voice demanded behind her.

She spun around to see the man that she'd run into when getting on the elevator. At that moment she lost control of the deck of cards she was still shuffling and they went flying into the air, several of them smacking him in the chest.

~

It was hard for Rabbi Jeremiah Silverman not to worry about Cindy. He hated that she no longer worked next door. Not only did he not get to see her most days for lunch but he also couldn't keep tabs on her. He liked being with shouting distance in case something went wrong. It wasn't paranoia, bad things did happen to Cindy. He just wanted to make sure he was always there when they did.

Ever since they'd become engaged it seemed like their lives had been turned upside down even more than usual. He knew she didn't like doing all the temp jobs and he didn't like it either. Most of the assignments were short, far too short to run any kind of proper background check on her coworkers. She had made him promise not to do that after the first time, but still.,,

His office door slammed open, startling him. Detective Mark Walters was standing, framed in the doorway. Behind him, looking nonplussed was Jeremiah's overbearing and usually overprotective secretary, Marie.

Jeremiah raised an eyebrow. "Does he have an appointment I'm not aware of?" he asked, directing his question to Marie.

"No, he does not," she said with a sniff. "He insisted on barging in here and there was nothing I could do to stop him."

He smiled at her. "It's fine. Hold my calls, though, until the Detective leaves."

Marie scowled but gave a short nod before stalking off.

"Well, come in and tell me what's got you so upset," Jeremiah said to Mark.

The detective slammed the door behind him and stalked up to Jeremiah's desk. His aggressiveness was unusual and one look at his face told Jeremiah that his friend was upset.

"What can I do for you?" he asked.

"I'm here to talk to you about something important," Mark said roughly.

"What is it?" Jeremiah asked, growing concerned.

"I need you to do something for me," he said, his voice ominous.

"And what exactly do you want me to do?"

Mark locked eyes with him. "I need you to kill someone."

2

Jeremiah lunged out of his chair and moved around the desk.

"Quiet," he hissed at Mark, pulling him farther away from the door.

His heart was pounding as he was wondering what kind of trouble Mark had gotten himself into that he'd make that kind of a request of him. He looked at his friend. The detective was more than agitated, he was exhausted. His eyes were bloodshot, his skin was pale. He looked like he hadn't slept in days.

Jeremiah put a hand on his shoulder and then shoved him down onto the couch. Mark's legs collapsed beneath him and he fell with a grunt. Jeremiah crouched down in front of him.

"Look at me, Mark," he said.

The detective was staring moodily at the ground and didn't lift his eyes.

"Look at me!" Jeremiah snapped.

Mark's head jerked upward and he met Jeremiah's stare.

"Okay, tell me who you want...dead," he said.

Mark took a deep, shuddering breath. "That no good, unreliable, betrayer."

"And that would be?" Jeremiah asked.

"My sorry excuse for a partner."

"Liam? You want to kill Liam?" Jeremiah asked surprised.

"Kill him dead," Mark said solemnly.

~

Cindy flushed. "I'm so sorry," she said, crouching down to pick up her scattered cards.

"Are you always this clumsy?" the man demanded.

Are you always this rude? she wanted desperately to ask. Instead she just shook her head. She finished picking up her cards and stood up.

"I'm Cindy Preston, your new temp."

He was staring at her with narrowed eyes. She was surprised to realize that he was about her age. She had the impression of someone older. She realized after a moment it was the expensive suit and arrogant bearing that made him seem older. He would have been a handsome man if it wasn't for the scowl plastered on his face.

I have a friend who could buy and sell you a hundred times over, she thought to herself. Then she gave herself a mental nudge and forced a smile. She wasn't going to make this any better by meeting his rudeness with hostility of her own.

"Okay," he finally said. "Follow me."

He turned and walked out of the office and she scurried behind. He passed Leo without even acknowledging him, though Leo, for his part, was watching Mr. Cartwright closely.

Her new boss stopped at the cubicle next to Leo's. There was no one in it and the computer monitor was dark. There were, though, papers and personal effects scattered all around.

"This is where you'll be working," Mr. Cartwright said.

"It looks like someone is already sitting here," Cindy said.

If anything Mr. Cartwright's scowl just deepened. "Not anymore. When we hire a permanent employee they'll take over this spot from you. Now, I'll see you in my office in half an hour. I have a letter I want you to send out."

He turned and strode away. Cindy sat down in the chair and it spun slowly.

Well, that could have gone better, she thought. *At least half of it is my fault. I should just suck it up and try to get along.*

She didn't want to. She hated the building. She hated the look and feel of it. She hated that she was sitting at a desk filled with someone else's trinkets. She was pretty sure if given half a chance she'd hate her new boss, too.

God, give me strength, she prayed.

She had been surprised to discover just how much she missed working at the church. With all its craziness and the potential for drama at any moment there had still been something special about knowing she was part of something like that. She had felt like she was serving God. It was funny, she'd initially taken the job there out of necessity and because it seemed like the least odious of the job positions she'd interviewed for. Now she found she was actually attached to it.

It wasn't just the people, many of whom she still interacted with. It wasn't just the building, heaven knew it was nice not to have to worry about whether all the sinks and toilets were in working order come Monday morning.

"Hey, you okay?"

She snapped out of her reverie and turned to see Leo standing up and looking down at her over the partition.

"Yeah, I'm fine," she said, forcing another smile.

"Good."

He sat back down and she turned her focus to her nightmarishly messy desk. It was a stark contrast with the neatness of her boss's desk. She opened a drawer of the desk, planning to shove her purse in. The drawer was stuffed with papers and all sorts of odds-and-ends so it seemed. She tried the next two drawers with similar results. Finally she put her purse under her desk.

If she was really going to be working here for a few weeks then she needed to get things cleaned up so she'd be able to work. She glanced at a picture frame sitting next to the computer monitor. It held a picture of a beautiful young woman who was wearing a rose in her hair and smiling at the camera. She had her arm around an older woman who could easily have been her grandmother.

Cindy frowned. The frame was nice and the picture was very intimate. She wondered why its owner had left it behind. She glanced slowly around the desk and noticed all the other things that had been left behind.

There was a red stapler that had the name Rose written on it in rhinestones. Cindy smiled. That was one way to make sure your coworkers didn't constantly make off with your stapler, especially if you worked with a lot of men.

A brightly decorated stained glass votive holder was the home for several pens with bright, fake flowers attached to their ends. Sitting altogether they looked like a pretty little bouquet. It was a bit of cheer in an otherwise drab building.

There was a little stuffed unicorn with a heart on its flank. A gold rose pendant necklace was draped over the edge of the computer monitor. There was more. Whoever had sat here before her had worked to make this cubicle her own.

She should get a box to put all these things in. Surely their former owner, Rose she was guessing, would want them. Why she hadn't taken them already was beyond Cindy. When she'd quit she'd taken all her personal items from her desk at the church.

She'd find one after her meeting with the boss. She had a few minutes so she began to stack papers. She started to look at them but realized it was going to take quite a while to figure out what she needed to do with each of them. She found an inbox, half buried under some paper and a sweater that was perched on top. She barely managed to stuff the sweater in one of the overflowing drawers. Then she was able to start stacking all the paper in the inbox to be gone over later.

When half an hour was up and it was time to go to the meeting she was still feeling overwhelmed by the amount of clutter and work that it represented, but at least she had carved out a couple of bare spots of desk to work on until she could get everything more organized.

She grabbed a notepad she'd found. She thought of taking one of the flower pens but ultimately settled on a black pen with gold lettering that she found hiding amongst the others. She headed back to Mr. Cartwright's office. The door was closed and she knocked.

"Enter," she clearly heard him say.

She walked in and moved to take the seat across the desk from him.

"Shut the door," he said without looking up from a paper he was perusing.

Cindy hesitated. She wasn't comfortable being in a closed room with a man she didn't know. She was about to voice her objection when she realized he probably wouldn't care how it looked or how she felt.

She got up and went back over to the door. She closed it most of the way, leaving it slightly ajar. That way if she needed help it should be easy for someone to hear her screaming.

You're so paranoid! she lectured herself as she returned to her seat. *He's not a criminal, he's your boss. Honestly what's wrong with you?*

Her inner critic was having a field day making her feel like an idiot. She got as comfortable as she could in the chair and waited expectantly. He'd said he needed to send a letter. That seemed like a simple thing unless he needed to have it sent registered mail or something like that.

"To all personnel," he said, beginning to speak without looking up. "It has come to my attention that the time clock in the south entrance broke on or around March second and nobody bothered to give management proper notice."

Cindy scrambled to start writing on her notepad as she realized that he was dictating a letter to her. Why on earth he didn't just type it up himself she had no idea, but a moment later was too busy writing to think about it anymore.

"As a result, all employees who clocked in at the south entrance will have their records checked, and if appropriate, their pay docked for any time the company was shorted."

He kept going, droning on as she struggled to keep up. She'd never taken dictation before and it was challenging. She abbreviated wherever she could. When at last he had

15

finished he finally looked up at her.

"Now, Cindy, I need you to go type that up and bring it back to me to read over. Is that clear?"

"Yes."

"Okay, you may go."

Cindy rose and hurried toward the door. She threw it open and breathed a small sigh of relief. Before leaving, though, she turned.

"The girl who was sitting at my desk before, I think her name was Rose, left a lot of personal items behind. If you like I could box them up and mail them to her if you have her address."

"No," he said quickly. "Bring them to me. I'll take care of mailing them."

"Are you sure? Because-"

"I said, 'bring them to me'," he reiterated, his voice tight.

"Okay," she said.

She left and went back to her desk. His response seemed odd to her, but Rose and her things would have to wait until after she finished typing up a letter. She turned on the computer monitor and was immediately prompted for a password.

"Dang it," she muttered under her breath.

~

Jeremiah passed a hand over his face. "Exactly what did Liam do to upset you this much?" he asked Mark.

"You mean what didn't he do," Mark said.

"Okay, what didn't he do?" Jeremiah asked.

"I'll tell you what he didn't do. He didn't pick me up

16

this morning for work," Mark burst out, clearly agitated.

Jeremiah stared at him, sure there had to be a lot more to it than that. He wasn't sure what was wrong or exactly what had tipped Mark over the edge, but it was starting to upset him a little. That was never a good thing.

"Maybe you should start from the beginning," he suggested.

Mark nodded doggedly. "You remember a few weeks ago, that juror who got killed, his jury summons stolen?"

"It's a bit hard to forget."

"The woman who witnessed it is Rebecca Thyme. She owns the Tea Thyme shop."

"Okay."

"Liam went moony eyed over her straight off. I told him he couldn't date a suspect and you know what he said?"

"I can't imagine," Jeremiah said.

Mark snorted. "He said there was no harm in him dating a witness."

"So, Liam is dating Rebecca?" Jeremiah asked, struggling to see how this had anything to do with anything.

"Yes, although he doesn't like to admit it. I don't know why, but he's dating her all the same. I know."

"Well, you are a detective."

"That's right."

If Jeremiah didn't know better he'd swear Mark was intoxicated. The more he observed him, though, the more convinced he was that the other man was suffering from sleep deprivation. Twin infants in the house could do that to anyone, he supposed.

"So, he's dating Rebecca," Jeremiah prompted.

"Yeah, she gained a boyfriend and I lost a partner,"

Mark said despondently. "He keeps forgetting things, leaves me to deal with messes so that he can go spend more time with her. I've done more paperwork in the last four weeks, mine and his. We were at a crime scene last week and he nearly contaminated it by forgetting to put on his gloves before going to pick up a piece of evidence. He's losing it. The only thing he can focus on is her. His work's suffering. *Our* work's suffering. I can't even get him to focus long enough to discuss cases with him. He just drifts off, all obsessed with her. And now, today, the ultimate insult. He didn't pick me up for work."

"Don't you usually drive your car?" Jeremiah asked.

"Not today. It's in the shop. I told him that five times yesterday, reminded him that he needed to pick me up for work. So, I waited and waited this morning. I called him and called him and he didn't even have the courtesy to pick up the phone. He's probably taking her flowers or bringing her coffee. He likes to do that in the mornings. Then he gets sucked in, though. Two minutes become two hours. He's completely irresponsible!"

"Sounds like he's in love," Jeremiah said softly.

Mark snorted. "That's no excuse."

"Don't you remember what it was like when you and Traci started dating? I'm sure you became just as...crazy trying to spend every second with her."

"That was different. When I met Traci I wasn't a detective. I didn't have the responsibilities he does," Mark ranted.

"It seems to me that you need to just relax and cut him a little bit of slack. It's still new for him. Give it a while and I'm sure you'll get your caring, *supportive* partner back," Jeremiah said, putting special emphasis on the last part. He was sure that if Mark weren't so exhausted he would see the sense of that rather than fly off the handle like he did.

"I doubt it," Mark grumbled. "Trust me, though, one way or another I'm making him pay for today."

Jeremiah frowned. "How did you get here without your car?"

"I took Traci's," Mark said, indignity heavy in his voice.

"I don't think I've ever seen Traci's car," Jeremiah said with a frown.

"For good reason. I keep it locked in the garage," Mark said with a groan.

"Well, at least you have transportation, even if your car is in the shop. So, don't you think your reaction to Liam not showing up this morning was a little bit extreme?"

Mark rocketed to his feet, nearly knocking Jeremiah over. "Extreme? Extreme? You come with me right now," he said, heading for the door.

Jeremiah stood up and followed Mark, closing his door behind them. Marie looked up as Mark stormed past her desk and raised an eyebrow. Jeremiah just rolled his eyes and shrugged.

They made it to the parking lot and Mark stopped and extended his arm dramatically.

There in the parking lot was a pink car with cavorting horses of unnatural colors all over it. He stared at one pink horse with curly mane and tail that was a slightly different shade than the car itself.

"What is this?" he asked.

"She calls it the Ponymobile," Mark fumed. "She had the whole thing wrapped with My Little Pony. She was showing it to the kids and she became obsessed with it."

"Oh my."

"Yeah. Can you imagine? You know how cops are. When I show up in this-"

"You will never, ever stop being teased about it," Jeremiah finished.

"Exactly!"

"Why didn't you just take a taxi?"

"Couldn't. I've got a crime scene I'm supposed to be on my way to right now."

"Then why on earth are you here?" Jeremiah asked.

"Because someone had to know why before I find Liam and wring his neck. He's a dead man."

Jeremiah nodded slowly, not sure what else to say. Deep down he wanted so badly to laugh, but was afraid that would just send Mark over the edge he was already teetering on.

He knew it had been hard for Mark to regain the respect of his fellow police officers the past couple of years after having tortured a prisoner for information. This, though, he would never come back from. He'd be the pony guy for the rest of his life and then some.

Jeremiah was on the verge of telling Mark he could borrow his car when the detective's phone rang.

Mark yanked the phone out of his pocket. "What?" he demanded unceremoniously.

Jeremiah watched as Mark's already pale skin turned even paler. The man's hand started shaking as it held the phone.

"When?" Mark whispered.

"Is he..."

Mark ended the call and stood, staring, his hands still trembling. Finally he buried his head in them.

"What is it, Mark?"

"They found...they found him...he'd been attacked," Mark stammered.

"Who?"

"Liam."

3

"Mark, what did you do?" Jeremiah asked sharply.

Mark shook his head fiercely. "Not me."

"Where is he?"

"The hospital. A nurse at the front desk called. He's...he might not..."

"Come on, let's get there," Jeremiah said, heading toward his car. He reached it and turned back to Mark. "Move it, Detective!" he shouted.

Mark shook himself and lurched forward. He practically threw himself into the passenger seat as Jeremiah put the car in reverse.

Liam has been attacked. It doesn't look good.

The words he'd heard on the phone played and replayed in his head. They had been enough to knife through his haze of anger and exhaustion. He had been saying something horrible about Liam right before then, hadn't he?

He couldn't remember. He couldn't even remember why he'd been at the synagogue. All he could think about was his partner who had needed him.

I wasn't there for him.

He mentally screamed at himself to stop it. He didn't know what had happened. He didn't even know where Liam had been, what he'd been doing, or who had attacked him and why.

"Rabbi, I'd appreciate it if you'd pray," Mark said.

Seconds later he realized just how upset Jeremiah was, too, as the man started speaking rapidly in Hebrew. Mark wished he knew what the words meant. He focused on the sounds, the rise and fall, the inflection.

He should call Traci and tell her what was happening. And...there was something else...someone else.

Rebecca. He should call Rebecca and tell her.

He started to reach for his phone and then stopped. He didn't know what to tell either of them. They'd want, *need* the answers as badly as he did. He would find out what he could and then call them.

~

Cindy clicked on the field for username and it auto filled the name rosemeyer. She held her breath, hoping, as she clicked on the password field, but it remained blank.

She stood up. "Excuse me," she said.

Leo looked up at her.

"I'm trying to get into the computer. You wouldn't by any chance know her password would you?" Cindy asked.

It was a long-shot, but if he didn't then she'd ask him who to call for computer help.

"No, sorry. They make us change our password every two weeks," Leo said. "They say it's for security purposes."

"Okay, thanks," Cindy said.

That actually might be helpful. If it was always the same password Rose would have had it memorized. If she had to keep changing it, though, she might not have.

On a hunch Cindy opened the drawer that contained all

the paperclips, post-its, and other odds and ends. She pulled it all the way out. There, in the back was a tiny folded post-it note. She unfolded it and saw written on it: 2KC1222!

She turned and entered that in the password box. The screen blinked and then the computer pulled up the desktop. The screen was littered with icons for various files and programs. It was dizzying just looking at it.

As much of a jumbled mess as the drawers.

Fortunately the icon for Word was on the bottom toolbar. She clicked on it and a moment later it pulled up a partial file that said it was recovered from an unexpected shutdown. She stared at it, but quickly realized that it looked like a personal letter.

She was about to close it without saving, but out of habit saved the letter at the last second. She noted that the document title was KC. She opened a blank document and got busy typing up the letter for her boss. As she did so she couldn't help but wonder why he didn't type up his own letter. It would take less time than dictating it to her and having her do it. He was young enough that he should be extremely comfortable with computers. Maybe it just made him feel important to give the grunt work to someone else.

She realized that wasn't the most generous of thoughts. Then again, he had rubbed her the wrong way from the start. She sighed. It was going to be a long few weeks.

~

The hospital finally loomed in sight. Mark was already undoing his seatbelt when Jeremiah slid into a parking spot close to the emergency room. Mark was out of the car and running inside in the blink of an eye.

He ran up to the admittance nurse. "Liam O'Neill, how is he?" he gasped out.

Before the nurse could answer a small voice behind him said, "We don't know yet."

He spun around and saw Rebecca standing there, eyes red and puffy from crying. He took a step toward her. "What happened?"

At that moment Jeremiah arrived. Mark looked at him. "Jeremiah, this is Rebecca. Rebecca, Jeremiah."

Jeremiah nodded and Mark turned back to Rebecca.

"Liam called me at the shop to tell me that he was running a couple of minutes late but that he was bringing me a surprise. I waited and then I finally called him back and it just rang. I started to get a bad feeling and I walked outside toward where he usually parks. I found him, on the ground."

Her breath caught a bit in her throat. She balled her hands into fists and continued. "He had been beaten badly. He was unconscious. I called 911 and they let me ride over in the ambulance with him."

She was holding herself very rigidly. He suspected it was to keep herself from collapsing. Rebecca was tough. She'd served time in the military, doing two tours in Afghanistan. She also had her share of scars from that, mostly on the inside from what he could tell.

"Was there anything at the scene that would indicate who did this?" Mark asked.

She shook her head. "Not that I could see."

"We need to get a team over there to check it out," he said, feeling edgy. "It's a crime scene. There might be something that could tell us what happened."

"There was blood, although it might have all been Liam's," Rebecca said, turning paler.

Liam was a big guy, a strong guy. It was hard to imagine he'd gone down without a fight. He needed to call in and get a forensics team over there before the scene was completely compromised. He pulled his phone out of his pocket and stared at it, his mind whirring. He tried to tell himself to make the call, but it was like his fingers wouldn't obey him. And over and over in his mind he kept thinking *I'm going to lose another partner.*

"Stop it!" he rebuked himself out loud, startling all of them. "Sorry," he mumbled.

Suddenly a door opened and a doctor came striding through, face grim. Mark blanched. Liam hadn't been here very long. The news couldn't be good.

"You're here with Liam, the man who was beaten?" he asked.

They all nodded and the doctor ushered them over to a corner away from everyone else. Also not a good sign. Mark felt his chest tighten as he waited the next words with dread.

"I'll get right to it. He has internal bleeding. We're prepping him for surgery right now so we can go in and get it stopped. Beyond that we're looking at several broken ribs, his left arm is fractured, and he has a concussion in addition to all the cuts and bruises."

"Was there any blood or bruising on his knuckles?" Mark asked.

The doctor shook his head. "It looks like he didn't get in a single blow against whoever attacked him."

Mark blinked, trying to take that in. "So, someone took him by surprise."

The doctor shrugged. "That would be my best guess."

"When will you know if he's going to be alright?" Jeremiah interjected.

The doctor shook his head. "We should know more after the surgery."

"Thank you," Jeremiah said.

The doctor nodded then turned and left. The three of them stood there, staring at each other. Mark's phone rang and he looked down at it. It was the precinct calling.

"Hello?" he asked.

"Detective, what is your ETA at the crime scene?" a woman asked in clipped tones.

"Where Liam was attacked?" he asked, head still fuzzy.

There was a pause. "No, at the homicide, 32 Foster St. near Lexington. Officers on scene have been expecting you."

Mark blinked. That's where he and Liam were supposed to be. "Sorry, I...we have a situation. Liam was attacked, assailant unknown. He is in emergency and going into surgery," he said. "I just got to the hospital."

There was another pause on the other line. "Hold for a moment, please," she said, voice softer.

Mark held on, staring at the door where the doctor had disappeared as if somehow he would come running back through saying it was all a mistake and Liam was just fine, no surgery required.

"Detective?"

"Yes?"

"I'm sorry. We have no one else."

"Okay," Mark said, running his hand through his hair. "I'll head over there. We need a forensics team to the site of the attack on Liam, though."

"Where was that?" she asked.

"One second."

He handed the phone to Rebecca who told the dispatcher exactly how far from her shop she had found Liam. When she was finished she handed the phone back to Mark.

"I'm sorry, Detective," the woman told him before hanging up.

Mark pocketed his phone and looked at Jeremiah and Rebecca. "I have to go," he said, the words heavy on his tongue.

"That's okay. I'm sure he's going to be in there a while," Rebecca said.

"I'll make sure and stop by the scene after I take care of this other, to see that the techs are doing what they can."

Rebecca nodded then suddenly winced.

"What's wrong?" he asked.

"I just realized that I left my shop unlocked. I never went back after I found him. I used his phone to call 911. I wasn't opening for another hour so the closed sign is in the window, but I still don't like leaving it unlocked."

"I'll swing by and lock up for you," Mark said.

"Thank you. The keys are in my purse which is behind the counter," she said, face twisted up.

He nodded. "I'll be back as soon as I can. Meantime, call me if you hear...ugh."

"What?" Jeremiah asked.

"I don't have a cellphone," Rebecca said. "And after I called the ambulance I put Liam's back in his jacket pocket. I wasn't thinking. I'm sure there's a payphone or the nurse will let me call."

"Hold that thought," Jeremiah said.

He turned and quickly left, heading toward the parking lot.

"Where's he going?" Rebecca asked.

"Danged if I know," Mark said. "I hope he's not leaving. He's my ride."

Jeremiah reappeared less than a minute later. He walked up and put a phone in Rebecca's hand.

"It's prepaid. I put Mark's number in there and mine," he said. "Call the moment you hear anything."

"Thanks, I will," she promised, closing her hand tight around the phone.

"Do you need anything?" Mark asked, still feeling lost.

"No, just go and take care of what you need to. And thanks for locking up the shop."

He nodded and then headed for the parking lot, Jeremiah beside him. As soon as they were inside the rabbi's car Mark turned to him. "Did you just give her a burner phone?"

"Yes."

"How many of those do you have?"

"A few, where I can get to them," Jeremiah said.

"How long has that been going on?" Mark asked.

Jeremiah gave him a look, the kind of look that said stop-asking-questions. The rabbi sighed, though, and put the car in reverse. "I've always had one. Since July I've had...more."

"Good to know," Mark said, at a loss for what else to answer.

"Where are we going?"

"I've got to get my car so I can get to work."

"No, your car is in the shop. Traci's car is in the synagogue parking lot where it's staying until you're ready to go home. What's the address of the crime scene?"

"It won't look good, me getting a civilian to drive me to a crime scene," Mark groused.

"Would you rather show up in the Ponymobile?"

"You're right. Take me to 32 Foster Street near Lexington."

"I'll drop you off and then I'll head to Rebecca's shop and take care of things there."

Mark started to bristle. It was his partner's girlfriend, his responsibility. Then he rubbed his forehead with his fingers. He was tired. It was logical. That way they didn't leave Rebecca's shop vulnerable longer than necessary. Plus the rabbi could make sure that the crime scene guys arrived in a timely fashion.

"Thank you," he said.

"That's what family is for," Jeremiah said, his voice kinder than Mark had ever heard it.

He held back a sob. It had only been a few months since he told Jeremiah he was like a brother to him. He had never really expected to hear the other man parrot it back to him. Given how tired and upset he was it was a welcome reminder that no matter what he wasn't alone. He had Traci. He had Jeremiah and Cindy.

"How is Cindy doing?" he asked.

Jeremiah grunted. "I hate her working temp jobs."

"Okay. Does she hate her working temp jobs?"

"Yeah, but she's trying to put on a brave face."

"That was a helluva thing she did quitting her job that way because the pastor was opposed to your relationship."

"Yeah. Don't remind me."

"Why, I might have to investigate the pastor's murder otherwise?" Mark joked.

As soon as the words were out of his mouth he was horrified. That wasn't funny. He glanced quickly at Jeremiah who was staring fixedly at the road ahead. The rabbi's hands were wrapped so tightly around the steering wheel that Mark couldn't help but think he was symbolically trying to crush the life out of it.

"I can't just kill everyone who pisses me off," Jeremiah said.

A shiver ran up Mark's spine. It didn't sound like a matter-of-fact statement so much as a mantra the other man was repeating to convince himself of that.

"No, you can't." He winced again. That had come out more forcefully than it should have. "I'm sorry. I'm tired."

"It's not your fault," Jeremiah said.

For that Mark was immensely grateful. He would never want to be on the receiving end of fault when it came to Jeremiah.

"Do you know where Rebecca's tea shop is? Tea Thyme?" he asked, hurriedly changing the subject.

"Yes. It's not that far from where I'm dropping you off."

"Okay, good," Mark said, turning to stare out the window.

Silence fell and that was worse because he was left alone with his own thoughts which were all dark and turbulent.

"You're not going to lose him," Jeremiah spoke up suddenly.

"Excuse me?"

"Liam. He's strong. He comes from a tough family. He'll be fine."

"I hope so. How do you know that about his family?"

31

Mark asked.

"The stories he chooses not to tell just as much as the ones he does tell," Jeremiah said.

He pulled over to the curb. "We're here," he said.

Mark turned forward and saw the yellow police tape three houses up and the uniformed officers walking around. He sighed. Death. It was inescapable. "Here we go again."

He got out of the car and Jeremiah drove off. Mark took a moment, trying to compose himself. There was no telling who he was going to encounter on scene and he had to be professional and stay alert to whatever he uncovered.

He took a step forward just as a bloodcurdling scream ripped through the air.

4

Mark raced forward just in time to see officer Taylor holding back a young woman at the front door. She was fighting him, clearly trying to get inside.

"Miss! Please calm down!" Taylor was begging. "You don't want to go in there."

"My parents are in there!" she wailed. "What's happening?"

"There's been an...accident," he said hesitantly.

She stopped struggling. "What kind of accident?"

Taylor let go of her. Before Mark could shout a warning she'd leaped past the startled man. They both ran in after her. She stopped short just inside the kitchen and screamed again.

A man and a woman's bodies were on the ground, their heads smashed in. Next to them, sitting, cradling a blood covered baseball bat and rocking back and forth was a teenage boy with pale skin and a shock of dark hair. He was moaning to himself.

"What did you do?" the young woman asked, clearly addressing the boy. "What did you do?" she shouted when he didn't answer her.

He didn't look up, just kept cradling the bat and rocking.

"He's been like that since we got here," Taylor said softly.

Mark put a hand on her shoulder. "Miss, I need you to come in the other room with me."

She went. The shock was beginning to set in and she was easy to lead to the living room where she collapsed onto a chair as though her legs couldn't hold her up any more.

Mark crouched down next to her. "What's your name?" he asked.

"Ruth," she said numbly.

"Okay, Ruth. I'm Detective Walters. Were those your parents in there?"

She nodded.

"Okay. Is the boy your brother?"

She nodded again.

"What's your brother's name?"

"Casey, you know, like the poem, Casey at the Bat." A shudder passed over her and tears began to slide down her cheeks. She sobbed and dropped her head down. "Is he going to be okay?" she asked.

Mark licked his lips. He hadn't had a chance to talk to the officers already on scene before him but things looked bad. "Can you tell me what's wrong with him?" he asked gently.

"Casey...Casey is...he's developmentally delayed. He's also autistic."

"Okay, do you know the name of any of his doctors?" Mark asked. The sooner they got a medical professional out there to help, ideally one that Casey already knew and vice versa, the better it was going to be for everyone.

"Yes."

She lapsed into sobs and Mark put his hand on her shoulder, letting her cry for about half a minute before he tried again.

"Ruth, can you please give me the name of his doctor?"

Taylor came into the room, looking even more upset than Ruth did. The man was pale and shaking slightly. Sweat stood out on his forehead. Mark wasn't sure what was wrong with him, but he already had his hands full with Ruth.

"Dr. Milner," she finally got out.

Mark nodded to Taylor. "Get him down here," he said quietly.

The other officer pulled out his phone and left the room. Mark got up, found a bathroom, and grabbed a handful of tissues. He returned and handed them to Ruth who took them gratefully.

"Ruth, I know this is hard, but I need to ask you some more questions," Mark said.

She blew her nose on one of the tissues and then nodded.

"When you came in the kitchen, you asked Casey what he'd done. What did you mean by that?"

"I-I," she stammered, turning bright red. "I don't know."

She clearly didn't want to tell him that her initial thought was that her brother had killed their parents.

"Has Casey ever been...violent?"

"Sometimes, I guess. He can throw tantrums, particularly when things aren't going his way."

"How do things not go his way?"

"It's mostly stuff related to...I mean, he gets upset when his schedule gets thrown off. He needs things to be predictable."

"And when they're not, does he get upset?"

She nodded.

He changed tactics. "Is that Casey's bat?" he asked.

She shook her head. "Casey doesn't have a baseball bat. There's only one baseball bat in the house and it belongs to our parents."

"So, that's their bat?" he prodded.

"I don't see how it could be. They keep it in a display case in the dining room."

"Can you show me?"

She hesitated. "It's on the other side of the kitchen."

"That's okay. You just sit here and I'm going to go check on it. I'll be right back."

Mark walked back to the kitchen. He gave Casey a wide berth and headed into the dining room. Once there he stopped and looked around. There was a lot of baseball themed artwork on the walls. The parents must have been real enthusiasts. A china cabinet held some figures and a couple of balls on display instead of the usual dishes.

He froze as his eyes passed over it to a hutch on the far side of the room. There was what looked like a stand that could hold a baseball bat in the horizontal position. It was sitting amidst the shattered remains of a glass case. He stepped forward carefully. Ruth had been right about the display case, but wrong about the bat still being in it.

Above the case on the wall was a picture and a letter with a seal of authenticity. He perused it and then whistled low.

"Did you say something, Detective?" one of the officers asked, peering into the room.

"Come take a look at this," he said.

The other man walked over and Mark indicated the letter. "I think the murder weapon may be even more significant than we thought."

"How so?"

"There was a baseball bat in this case before someone smashed it. According to this letter, it was incredibly valuable. It was signed by Babe Ruth."

"Wow."

"Yeah. Wow. Make sure they dust all this for prints. I want to be sure we know who smashed the case," Mark said.

He made his way back into the living room and sat down across from Ruth.

"Your parents own a bat signed by Babe Ruth?" he asked.

She nodded. "It's their pride and joy. Or, was, I guess. They loved that thing. They loved it more than...anything."

A bitter note crept into her voice at the end.

"They named your brother for the baseball poem. I'm guessing they named you for Babe Ruth?"

"That's right," she whispered.

"A family of baseball fanatics," he mused.

"Not a family, just them. I hate baseball. Casey doesn't care about it. Of course, that broke them up, just like...everything did. They thought they'd have a son who grew up to be a famous baseball player, you know?"

She was rambling, her anger and grief all rolled into one and spilling out indiscriminately. That was fine. You could often learn a lot more by just listening to someone in the aftermath of a tragedy than by trying to ask them a lot of questions.

"Nope. We were both disappointments," she said heatedly.

She glanced up at him and then hurriedly back down

again. She became fixated on the tissues wadded up in her hand.

"Do you think your brother took the bat?" Mark asked.

She shrugged.

"Do you think he hit them with it?"

"No! I mean, maybe, I don't know. I don't know anything anymore," she said. She started crying again and Mark eased back, giving her a moment. He had more questions and even if it took a while they would eventually get through all of them.

~

Cindy handed her new boss the letter she'd just typed up. "Here's the letter you dictated," she said, trying to keep her voice pleasant.

He didn't say anything and after a few seconds she turned to go.

"Wait, I didn't dismiss you," he said.

She turned back, biting her tongue to keep from snapping at him. She stood there and he picked up the letter. He began to read it over, his brow puckering.

"The second paragraph is no good, it will have to be reworked," he said, handing it back to her.

"Okay, what would you like me to say?" she asked.

He looked up at her and glared. "Don't ask me, just go fix it and bring it back."

She stood there for a moment, stunned. It was his own words he was objecting to. How did he expect her to fix it?

He waved his hand at her, as though shooing her out of his office. Infuriated she turned and walked out, nearly slamming the door behind her.

She made it back to her desk and sat down with a frustrated sigh.

"I'm sorry," she heard Leo say from the cube next door. "Thanks."

"Let me guess. He hates his own writing."

"Apparently."

"I hate to tell you this, but he's likely to hate your writing even more."

"Gee, thanks," she said, sarcasm dripping from her words.

"Just a heads up. I'd hate to have you march back in there thinking everything was going to be all better once he saw how you turned his drudgery into poetry."

She actually laughed a little at that. "Well, I'm not sure this memo could be turned into poetry even by an expert."

"You'd be surprised what a great poet or artist can do with trash. In fact, I hear that there are fancy art galleries in the big cities that have displays of trash and charge quite a lot for them."

Cindy smiled. "Maybe I'll just crumple this up, glue it to a piece of wood, and title it 'Ode to Corporate Time Wasting'."

"And you said you weren't a poet," Leo teased.

At least there was one person in the place who wasn't a total jerk. She took a deep breath. That wasn't fair. She'd only really met three, counting the security guard. Hopefully there were more people like Leo than like that guy and Mr. Cartwright.

She opened up the Word document and set about trying to polish the second paragraph. There wasn't a lot that could be done with it, but at least she'd give it her best shot. She owed it to corporate poets everywhere.

~

Jeremiah was worried about Mark. The detective was fraying around the edges and it was only a matter of time before he lost it and did something stupid or negligent. What made things worse was that he wasn't sure how he could help him. He needed to figure out a way to help Mark, though, or risk losing his friend to the darkness that so often devoured those pushed past their limits.

Thanks to the events of the morning he was now also worried about Liam. The Irishman was tall, strong, and not the kind to go down without a fight. That and the absence of bruising on Liam's hands suggested to Jeremiah that whoever had attacked him had caught him off guard and knocked him out before beating him. Something that vicious pointed toward someone with a grudge and probably a history of violence. It could be a random act of violence, but Jeremiah's gut told him otherwise.

The attack could be work related. Someone Liam had put away could be out and looking for payback or be angry enough to have someone else exact revenge for him. If that was the case then Mark could be in danger as well since the two were partners. Of course, it could also be related to an arrest Liam made before he became a detective. Jeremiah would have to ask Mark if anyone who might bear a grudge against either of them had been recently released. That wouldn't do anything to ease the detective's anxiety, unfortunately.

The other option was that this was not job related and entirely personal. The big man was friendly, outgoing, and also had a lot he didn't share about himself and his family.

It was obvious to Jeremiah. He was fairly certain that Liam himself had nothing to hide. He wasn't sure the same could be said for his kin. Sometimes family baggage found a way to land on the one person who didn't deserve it.

He decided that after he swung by the shop he would see if he could find the place where Liam had been attacked and try to glean anything he could. That was if the police didn't get there first and tape off the scene or accidentally destroy clues.

He briefly thought about doing that first, but it would only take him a minute to go to Tea Thyme and lock up. The site of Liam's attack would be close by and he might glean something by walking the path Rebecca had when she went to find Liam.

He parked about half a block from the shop. Liam's car was there and Jeremiah parked several spaces away from it. Jeremiah began to carefully scrutinize everything as he got out of his car. From the shop there was no line of sight to Liam's car or the sidewalk that he would have been walking on once he parked.

Jeremiah walked in the street, keeping close enough to the sidewalk to look for tell-tale blood stains but staying far enough away to hopefully keep from contaminating the scene. He was surveying the scene as he walked, but his objective was still to go lock up the shop first before giving the area a thorough examination.

The first thing he found, though, stopped him in his tracks. It wasn't on the sidewalk. Rather it was on the cement parking bumper that was a few inches away from the curb. There were bloody streaks on it as though someone had wiped their shoes on it to free them of the liquid.

Jeremiah glanced up at the sidewalk. Five feet further on he saw the bloodstained concrete where Liam had fallen and been beaten. Anger flared inside him and he clenched his fists, struggling to keep it in check.

The marks on the concrete barricade were on the side away from the sidewalk. They stretched far enough along it that he could surmise that either there had been no car parked in the space at the time of the incident or there had been something very narrow there such as a motorcycle.

Jeremiah cast his eyes back toward the street. There was a single skid mark there that looked fresh. He moved over to it, bent down, and could smell the unmistakable scent of burnt rubber. A single track such as that was definitely a motorcycle, likely someone speeding away.

He gave the spot a wide berth and moved to where he could observe the sidewalk. There was indeed a sizeable pool of blood. Aside from that the only thing he could see that was out of place was a few yellow rose petals on the ground nearby.

Rebecca said that Liam had told her he was bringing her something. Was it flowers? If so, where had they gone? She hadn't had anything like that with her in the waiting room. It was possible someone could have come by and picked up a bouquet. Although the blood nearby would scare off most people.

He turned and glanced up the street. There wasn't a lot of traffic this time of morning. There weren't any nearby buildings with obvious cameras that could show them what had happened. The forensics team should be arriving soon if they weren't already swamped somewhere else.

He decided to walk the rest of the short distance to her shop and lock up. A few quick strides brought him to the front door which was closed. The sign in the front window declared the store as open. He frowned. Rebecca must have forgotten that she had flipped it over. He pulled the door open and stepped inside.

He reached for the open sign to turn it over, but his hand froze an inch from it. His eyes probed the room quickly. Someone had been there before him. The place had been searched.

5

Jeremiah stood just inside the shop and looked around as he debated his options. The logical thing to do would be to alert the police, or at least to let Mark know to do so. Without Rebecca there it wouldn't be easy for them to tell if anything was missing. He had a feeling that it would be hard to pull her away from the hospital, though, until she knew Liam was going to be okay.

He moved gingerly into the room and rounded the counter. Her purse was where she'd said it would be, but it had clearly been rifled through. He couldn't help but wonder if the attack on Liam had been a grudge against him or just a ploy to lure Rebecca away from the shop.

He shook his head. Whoever had done this could have gone through her shop the night before or early that morning without having to put a policeman in the hospital. While it seemed likely the two incidents were connected he couldn't rule out the possibility that someone had come to her shop, realized that no one was there, and rummaged around looking for something to steal. He wanted to check her purse to see if her money and credit cards had been stolen but he didn't have gloves with him and he couldn't risk obliterating any fingerprints the intruder might have left behind.

He pulled out his cell phone and called Mark. The detective didn't answer. He must have his hands full at the crime scene Jeremiah had dropped him off at. He left a terse message and then called the burner phone he'd left with Rebecca.

"Hello?" she answered.

"Hi, it's Jeremiah. I have some bad news. I'm at your shop and someone has searched it. It looks like they went through all your drawers and cabinets and they searched your purse as well."

"What?! Did they take anything?"

"I can't tell that. I'm going to let the police know so they can check for fingerprints. Until then I'm not going to touch anything. You need to be here to help them figure out what's missing."

"But Liam-"

"Would be the first person to tell you that you need to help the police as quickly as you can so whoever did this can be found...especially if it's the same person who attacked him."

"You think they could be connected?" she asked, her voice shaking slightly.

"I think the timing is suspicious," he said.

Which was true, and she really did need to be here to speak with the police as they went through her shop. He knew that if he was in her shoes the only thing that would move him from that hospital was the possibility of catching the person who had put his loved one in there.

"I'm going to wait until the police get here and then I'll come pick you up and bring you here. Then I'll go back to the hospital and call you the second there's any news."

"Okay," she said reluctantly.

"Alright. I'll be there shortly."

He hung up. He tried calling Mark back and this time

the detective answered.

"What is it?" he asked, his voice on edge.

"Someone's been in Rebecca's shop before I got here. The place has been searched. You're going to need the forensics team to go over things here as well as outside."

"Lovely," Mark said sarcastically. He sighed. "Fine, give me a minute."

"I told her that I'd come pick her up so she can help the police figure out what might be missing," Jeremiah said.

"Good."

"Everything okay?"

"Things are...messy...here," Mark said.

That was not a way in which Mark normally described things. It piqued his curiosity but now was not the time to press for details. "Okay, call me if you need something."

"Thanks," Mark said.

Jeremiah ended the call and then stepped back outside to wait for the police. Fortunately they arrived shortly. Jeremiah recognized one of the uniformed officers who he'd seen before at other crime scenes. The man walked straight up to Jeremiah.

"Detective Walters said you'd be waiting for us."

Jeremiah nodded and indicated the shop. "I entered and discovered that the place had been searched prior to my arrival."

"Did you touch anything?"

"Only the door."

Two more officers were busy setting up a barricade around the blood-stained sidewalk where Liam had been attacked.

"There's blood stains also on the one concrete parking bumper and fresh tire tread on the ground," Jeremiah said, unable to help himself. He hated having to share the things he observed with the police. Ordinarily he would have confided only in Mark and let him handle things, but today was different. Mark wasn't here and he owed it to Liam to do all that he could to help ensure his attacker was found.

"Thanks. Always good to have you around," the officer said offhandedly.

Jeremiah winced inwardly. Those kind of observations by others were what he tried to avoid. Honestly at this point he wasn't sure why he even kept trying.

Because even though it feels like the whole world knows my secret in reality only six people do, he reminded himself. He didn't want that number growing so he had to remain careful, vigilant.

"I'm going to go pick up Rebecca, the owner, at the hospital and bring her back here," Jeremiah told the officer.

"Thanks, that will be very helpful," he said as he pulled a pair of gloves out of his pocket.

Jeremiah nodded and then hurried to his car before any of the other officers could engage him in conversation. Rebecca was the one who needed to be here, not him. The sooner he had her here the sooner he could relax a little.

The drive to the hospital was short and to her credit Rebecca was waiting just inside the emergency room door. As soon as he pulled up outside she ran out and got in his car.

"The sooner we get there the sooner you can get back here and stay on top of the doctors," she said, her voice tight.

Jeremiah nodded and hit the gas even as she was still buckling her seatbelt. "No word yet I take it."

"None," she said. "I just want to grab one of the nurses

and slap them until they talk."

"I doubt they know anything," Jeremiah said.

"Why do you think I haven't done it yet?" she asked tartly.

Jeremiah glanced at her sideways out of the corner of his eye. She was sitting, every muscle rigid. She dressed like one would expect the owner of a tea shop to dress, right down to ruffles on her blouse and the floral print on her skirt. She looked delicate, like fine bone china. It was his understanding, though, that she was former military. It was certainly showing in the way she was holding her spine and the steely resolve and aggression in her voice.

Offhand he'd say that Liam had found his match. A nice girl with refinement who could probably give him a run for his money in a fair fight. He hadn't had the opportunity to see them together but from what he knew of Liam and what he was observing of her, the extrapolations his mind was coming up with made a lot of sense.

"I'll stay on top of them once I get back to the hospital. If you want, I'll even rough up one of the doctors a bit," he said, his voice kind with a hint of teasing.

She turned to him sharply and stared at him intently before relaxing slightly into her seat. "Let's not escalate until they give us reason to," she said.

"Understood. Will save the enhanced interrogation until provoked."

She laughed. "Liam was right. You are interesting."

He forced himself to smile. "Well, you know, us interesting types have to stick together."

"I guess so," she said, sighing and then turning to stare out the window.

"The best thing you can do is give the police as much

detail you can about everything, including anything that was taken from your shop or even moved."

"I know the drill," she said. "Liam and I met because I saw a murder a few weeks ago."

"I am aware."

"Is Mark there?"

"No, he's at a homicide they were called to earlier this morning."

"I wish that's where Liam was right now."

"We all do."

"I can't help but think that if he hadn't come to see me before work-"

"Don't think that way. Especially not until we know what happened, who did this and why. For all we know the fact that he was attacked so close to where you were and that you came out looking for him could have even saved his life," Jeremiah told her.

That was, if it hadn't been a complete random crime. If someone had been targeting him it's possible that if they'd jumped him somewhere else they might actually have managed to kill him.

Assuming that had been the intent of the attacker. The beating was brutal enough that it was believable that was the intent.

Jeremiah tried to push the thoughts from his mind. There wasn't enough information to let his thoughts mull over in any rational way. His energy was best spent elsewhere until there was.

They arrived on the street where her shop was. Rebecca sucked in her breath as she saw the police cars and the tape cordoning off both the sidewalk and the entrance to her shop.

"So much for not scaring my customers," she said wryly.

He suspected that at the moment that was really the least of her worries. Still, no business owner wanted to see that tape declaring their business a crime scene. If any customers did drive by today the gossip it generated would probably be unbearable.

He let her out on the other side of her shop from where Liam was attacked.

"You still have the phone I gave you?" he asked.

She nodded as she closed the car door. She held up her right hand and he could see that it was clutched tightly in her fist.

"Call if you need me and I'll call you the second I hear anything."

"Thank you," she said.

She turned and headed to her store, ducking under the police tape.

Jeremiah's heart went out to her. She was having a rough day. A lot to process, too much, really. He just hoped that whatever she and the police discovered in her shop helped them find whoever was behind all this.

He headed back to the hospital, hoping that soon he'd have good news to share with everyone. They all needed it pretty badly, after all.

~

Mark had finished his preliminary questioning of Ruth when Dr. Milner arrived. The man was younger than he expected and he had a bushy reddish brown beard that seemed to draw the eye. The beard itself had two little braids in it making him look like some sort of character straight out of The Hobbit. Geanie would know which one. She'd invited everyone to celebrate her birthday a year earlier with what ended up being a nearly twenty-four-hour Tolkien marathon. Traci had loved it.

"Thank you for coming, Dr. Milner, I'm Detective Walters," Mark said, shaking the man's hand.

"How could I not when the officer explained what was happening?" the man asked, tension in every line of his body.

"I have to warn you, we haven't had a chance to move the bodies yet. We haven't wanted to disturb anything until we could get Casey out of there. There's not even sheets over them. If you like I'll see what we can do-"

"It's alright. I went to medical school. I've seen my share of cadavers," Dr. Milner said, interrupting.

Mark nodded. "Not quite like this, doctor. I just want to make sure that you're okay when you go in there."

"I do appreciate the concern, detective. I'm here to help Casey, though, and I can assure you that I will be able to focus one-hundred-percent on that until the job is done."

"Thank you for your candor."

"It's not a problem. I have to tell you that I don't believe him capable of the kind of violence described."

"You mean, he's never had any violent outbursts?" Mark asked, already knowing that wasn't the case from talking with Ruth.

"Outbursts yes, but limited to throwing things, screaming, that sort of thing. I have patients who hit. Casey has never been one of those."

"Thank you for your input. Hopefully we can figure out later exactly what Casey did or did not do. The important thing at the moment is to get him out of there and down to a room at the police station where we can get him cleaned up and hopefully talk to him."

Mark handed Dr. Milner a pair of gloves and the man put them on.

"Please, try to touch as little as you can while in there," Mark instructed.

Dr. Milner nodded. "Okay, let's do this."

Mark led the doctor down the hall and into the kitchen. He turned as the doctor stepped into the room and saw the man blanch as he took in the bodies on the floor. True to his word, though, he immediately turned his focus onto Casey. He knelt down next to the young man.

"Casey, it's Dr. Milner. I've come to see you," he said.

His voice was warm, friendly, calm. Mark had no idea how the man pulled that off under the circumstances. He was just grateful that he'd thought to call him in.

"We'll be just in the other room if you need us," Mark said, signaling the other officers present to clear out.

It was best to give the doctor some space to do what he had to. Mark left one officer in the hall where he could observe without being seen easily by Casey.

He headed back to the living room where he was intercepted by Taylor.

"Can I talk to you, sir?" Taylor asked, still looking the worse for wear.

"Sure," Mark said.

He followed Taylor outside and away from the house.

"What is it?" he asked when the other man finally stopped and turned to face him.

Taylor looked around as though trying to make sure no one else was watching.

"It's okay, I think we're alone," Mark said.

Taylor nodded and then drew his gun.

6

Fear rocketed through Mark and he raised his hands. "Easy there," he muttered.

His mind began to race. Taylor was a good cop. He'd dealt with him a few times before.

"It's okay," Mark said, trying to work out how to get the gun away from him and to get some help.

"It's not okay," Taylor hissed, face contorting.

"Whatever this is, we can work it out," Mark said.

"No! We can't."

"Listen-"

"No! You listen to me!"

"I'm listening," Mark hastened to reassure him.

Taylor was shaking, the gun barrel was bouncing back and forth and Mark did some quick calculations. If he could lunge to the side at just the right moment and hit Taylor's hand, he might send the gun flying without getting himself shot in the process.

"I need you to accept my badge and gun. I'm unfit for duty and I'm resigning as of right now," Taylor said fiercely.

Mark stared at him. That was the last thing he'd expected to hear the man say. "Lower the gun then," he finally managed to say in response.

Taylor instantly did so and Mark reached out and swiftly took it from him. After examining the gun for a moment he shoved it into the back of his waistband. With the gun secured he took a deep breath.

"Now, you want to tell me what's going on?" he asked.

Taylor abruptly sat down on the curb. After a moment's hesitation Mark joined him, sitting just out of arm's reach. The other man's shoulders slumped forward and he looked like someone who was utterly defeated.

"What happened?" Mark tried again.

"My partner and I got the 911 call," Taylor said after a minute. "No data, there was no one talking, it was just a call. We had no idea what we were walking into. Usually when there's silence like that someone's having a heart attack or something, you know? Fire truck arrived same time we did. We went in first."

Taylor stopped and a shudder seemed to pass over him.

"Was it your first homicide?" Mark asked, trying to figure out where the trauma was coming from. If it was his first, then Taylor was holding up better than most. Mark had a hard time believing it was, though, given how long Taylor had been on the force.

"No, sir, it wasn't," Taylor said. "I was first in the kitchen. I saw the wife first, her skull bashed in. Then I saw the husband."

"And?" Mark prompted when Taylor came to a stop again.

"Then I saw a guy crouched on the ground, holding a bloody baseball bat. He was jerking. I thought he was going to jump up and attack me. I pulled my gun and...and...I almost shot him," Taylor ended in a whisper.

Mark could feel the anxiety and fear rolling off the other man. The horror of nearly having killed someone who wasn't attacking him but who was in the middle of their own crisis.

"But you didn't shoot him," Mark said gently.

"I don't know why not. I was ready to. It was like at the last moment something froze my finger on the trigger and I didn't. It took me a couple more seconds to realize he wasn't a threat. He didn't even know that I was there."

"You do this job long enough and sooner or later you're going to find yourself in an impossible situation where you have to make a decision, often without all the facts. Just thank your lucky stars or God or your instincts or whatever that you made the right choice in the end."

"That's not good enough," Taylor said.

"I know, but that's what we get. Look, I'm not the one you can resign to and I know the captain. He'll insist you take a few days first to calm down before he'll accept it from you. So, do yourself a favor. Write up your report and then take the rest of the week off. Get out of town, go do some fishing, visit friends, whatever you do to feel better."

"Then what, come back, pretend it never happened?"

"You can't do that, but you learn from it, you add it to your experience bank and it helps you every time you come across an uncertain situation in the future."

"How did you come back and just carry on?" Taylor asked, lifting his head to look at Mark. His eyes were dark, his features pinched.

Mark blinked, sucking in his breath rapidly as though just struck. "I had the love of a good woman to help me and I reminded myself every day to learn from my experiences. And, I forgave myself."

He hated being reminded that the rest of his fellow officers hadn't forgotten what he'd done that one March day a few years back. As much as he tried to forget they never did and it came up at the most awkward times.

He stood. "I need to go see how the doctor's doing. You think about that time off, though."

"Thanks, Detective."

Mark turned and headed back into the house, doing his best not to fixate on his own shortcomings as he did so.

~

Jeremiah settled himself down in the waiting area at the hospital. He called Marie, explained where he was, and asked her to reschedule his one afternoon appointment which was with Ezra Abram, the rabbi that Cindy had met while serving on the jury a few weeks before. She had briefly voiced the thought about asking him to officiate their wedding. He had taken it upon himself to meet the man and get a feel for him before they discussed that any further.

The meeting could certainly wait a day or two, though. After all, if Cindy was serious about a December wedding the next year they had a little over a year-and-a-half to work some of these things out.

As he sat there waiting he wished he'd brought something to read with him. None of the magazines scattered around the room held any appeal for him. He wasn't in the mood to look at pictures of cats on his phone either, so he just sat and worked on stilling his mind, emptying it of turmoil and trying to order his thoughts.

He was finally starting to get somewhere when he heard a man say, "I'm looking for a rabbi."

Jeremiah looked up and saw a familiar looking man in his fifties, brown hair shot through with gray, talking to the nurse at the front. She frowned and started to shake her head.

Jeremiah cleared his throat and raised his hand. She saw him and said something to the man who turned quickly and walked toward him.

"Rabbi Silverman?"

"Yes," Jeremiah said, getting to his feet.

"I'm Rabbi Abram," the other man said, extending his hand.

Jeremiah nodded and shook it. "A pleasure to meet you, Rabbi."

"Please, call me Ezra," the other man said with a warm smile.

"If you'll call me Jeremiah."

"Of course, my son," Ezra said.

"What are you doing here?" Jeremiah asked, pleasantries over.

"Well, when your secretary called me to reschedule she told me you were waiting here for word on a friend. I figured I'd come and sit with you while you waited."

"You didn't have to do that," Jeremiah said, a bit taken aback.

"Nonsense, I wanted to. No one should wait for news like this by themselves."

Jeremiah was about to protest that there were others waiting for news, too, but decided against it. The older man was technically right. He was sitting and waiting alone, and it was tedious at best.

"Well, I appreciate it. Please, sit," Jeremiah said, pointing to the chair beside him as he retook his own seat.

"Thank you," Ezra said as he sat down. He made himself comfortable and then looked at Jeremiah with a twinkle in his eye. "I must say, young man, you've made quite a catch for yourself with Cindy," he said.

Jeremiah chuckled. "You are direct."

"Nothing if not," he said with a grin.

"How does that go over with your congregation?"

"They learn to love it or they go elsewhere," he said with a shrug. "It's not my job to coddle them. They have mothers for that."

Jeremiah couldn't help but chuckle again.

"So, what did you want to meet about?" Ezra asked.

"Cindy spoke highly of you. I figured I'd like to meet you."

Ezra stared at him intently for a long moment. Finally he spoke. "Just to be clear, I will perform an interfaith wedding, but I will put you both through holy hell before it."

It was not often that Jeremiah was surprised. It must have showed on his face because it was Ezra's turn to chuckle. "I know, too direct sometimes. This is what this is all about, though, right?"

"Cindy had a passing thought in that direction," Jeremiah admitted.

"I kinda thought that might be the case. Tell me, have you ever met a Messianic Jew before?"

"I can't say that I have."

"Uh huh. I thought so. You know, you're a bright guy and you're fixing to marry yourself a devout Christian. It seems to me you'd do well to at least ask me what I believe and why."

Jeremiah shook his head. "I've known Cindy for a few years now and she's never once tried to convert me. I've known you for two minutes and you're already there."

"What can I say? I'm not in love with you."

Jeremiah blinked at him. "You think that's the only reason she hasn't tried to convert me?"

"Probably not. Having met her I'd say she's not naturally the proselytizing type. But I'd allow that one reason she hasn't put her foot down more recently is she's too afraid to lose you."

Jeremiah struggled with how to respond to the other man. A number of emotions were swirling inside him and he couldn't focus on any one long enough to address it.

Ezra put a hand on his shoulder. "Look, I know I can be a bit much to take sometimes. But I like her, I really do. And looking at you I'm pretty sure that you're the one who's really terrified here. You're afraid of losing her. And, on some level, if I had to guess, I'd say you're afraid of dragging her down."

The emotions inside him sharpened and Jeremiah finally managed to ask, "How can you tell that?"

"You carry yourself like a man who has seen more than he should. Men like that often cling to a woman like Cindy like they're drowning, but are terrified of taking the girl under with them. I got a chance to observe Cindy pretty closely for a few days and I can tell you this, son, she's not going to break. She's tougher than even she knows and her love for you is one for the storybooks."

Ezra smiled kindly at him and Jeremiah took a shaky breath.

"Maybe we should talk more later," he finally managed to get out.

"I think that would be wise. Now, I'm glad to sit here and make small talk while you wait."

"I don't think you're capable of small talk," Jeremiah

accused.

"I don't know, try me, you might be surprised."

"Honestly, I'm not sure I could take any more surprises today."

"I can respect that," Ezra said, standing.

Jeremiah rose to his feet as well. The other rabbi held out his hand. "It's a pleasure to meet you, Jeremiah. I think you and I are going to have a lot to talk about."

Jeremiah shook his hand. "I wish I could say the feeling was entirely mutual," he said bluntly.

Ezra gave him a wink. "Eventually it will be."

He let go of Jeremiah's hand, turned and walked out of the emergency room. Jeremiah stood staring after him for a long minute. Ezra had hit more than a few nerves with his brief visit and pointed words. Jeremiah was entirely sure he never cared to have another conversation with the man again. He was equally sure that another conversation was somehow inevitable.

His stomach growled and he glanced at his phone. It was after lunch. He frowned. Cindy hadn't called him like she usually did. Hopefully everything was going okay at her new job. Maybe it was a good thing. Maybe she had made a friend to eat lunch with. Whatever it was he'd hear all about it that evening.

His stomach growled again and he thought about running down to grab something out of the vending machines in the cafeteria. The sandwiches in them were questionable to his mind, but he had no way of knowing how much longer before he heard something about Liam's condition.

As though somehow sensing his thoughts and deciding he had waited long enough, the door suddenly opened, and the doctor he'd seen that morning strode out, his face grim. Jeremiah's heart sank and he realized at that moment that he was the wrong person to be there. He wasn't Liam's family or his partner or his girlfriend. He was just a friend, not even an extraordinarily close one. They were friends because Liam was Mark's partner and as such was privy to certain information and truths.

Mark should be there or Rebecca. He didn't know where Liam's family lived and had no idea if anyone had thought to contact them. The doctor walked toward him, steps measured, eyes tired. He stopped in front of Jeremiah and put a hand on his shoulder.

"I'm so sorry," he began.

7

"Is he dead?" Jeremiah interrupted, unable to stand it any longer.

The doctor shook his head. "No, I'm sorry to keep you waiting so long. His injuries are extensive and we just now got him out of surgery. He's in post-op, In about an hour we'll have him in a room and you can see him."

"So, he's okay?" Jeremiah asked.

The doctor hesitated. "He's not entirely out of the woods. The next forty-eight hours will tell."

"So, what's wrong with him?" Jeremiah asked.

"We were able to get the bleeding stopped. There's been extensive trauma to his spleen as well as some trauma to his liver. There is hope that the injury to the spleen can heal, but we have to monitor him. If his blood pressure drops too low or there's more internal bleeding, we'll have to do another surgery to remove it."

Jeremiah nodded. He knew a ruptured spleen could kill a person.

The doctor continued, "Other than that he has five broken ribs and the left arm is fractures. He has a concussion. It looks like he was hit with something heavy in the back of his skull. Scans haven't revealed any signs of permanent injury or acute trauma to the brain, fortunately."

"Is he going to regain consciousness soon?"

"There's no reason to think that he won't as soon as the

anesthesia from surgery wears off. We'll keep him medicated to control the pain and to keep him from moving around too much until we see how things are looking."

"Thank you," Jeremiah said.

The doctor nodded. "I'll be in later tonight to check on him."

The doctor left. Jeremiah pulled out his phone and called Rebecca, who answered before he even heard it ring.

"He's out of surgery and in recovery. He can have visitors in about an hour," Jeremiah said without preamble. "The doctor said that there was damage to both his spleen and liver and the next forty-eight hours will be crucial. He should be awake a little later, though."

"Okay," she said, voice trembling.

"How are things at the shop?" he asked.

"We're still going over things here," she said.

He wasn't surprised. He knew from experience that the process of giving a simple statement to police could take an hour or more. With anything more complicated it just ballooned.

"Okay, let me know as soon as you need picked up," he said.

"Thanks, but I'll make one of them drive me to save time," she said.

"Sounds good. I'll let you know when I know the room number."

As soon as he hung up with her he called Mark. The detective sounded beyond frazzled but hopeful.

"Everything okay there?"

"Yeah, I'm wrapping up for now. We've got our suspect in custody. I've got to do a bunch of stuff at the station this afternoon. I want to see Liam first, though."

"How about I pick you up and take you to lunch? Then we can see him and afterwards I'll drop you at the station."

"That would be great."

"Okay, I'm on my way."

Jeremiah was relieved at the prospect of not having to eat at the hospital cafeteria. There were a lot of places close by where Mark and he could grab a quick bite. He headed outside, breathing in deep of the fresh air.

Mark was waiting for him outside the crime scene. He got in the car and they headed off.

"So you caught the killer?" Jeremiah asked.

"Looks as though."

"You're not completely sure?"

"When do we ever get that luxury?" Mark asked with a sigh.

More often than not from Jeremiah's perspective. He decided that saying so might be less than helpful at the moment so he stayed quiet.

"I mean if it looks like a duck, walks like a duck, and quacks like a duck..." Mark started then drifted off.

"Well, it's nice to have a quick resolution."

"Yeah," Mark said, still not sounding wholly convinced.

Jeremiah decided not to push. If Mark wanted to discuss it he would start talking about it on his own.

"Where do you want to eat?"

"Anywhere but Chinese food. We've had Chinese three nights in the last week."

"Okay, how about Italian?"

"Sure."

Jeremiah drove to Rigatoni's and a few minutes later the two of them were at a table waiting for their food.

"It really is straightforward," Mark started.

"What is?"

"The case. Developmentally disabled teen with autism, has a tantrum and kills his parents. Takes a baseball bat to each of their heads. Not just any bat either, a valuable one, signed by Babe Ruth."

Jeremiah raised an eyebrow. "Even I know that name."

"I would hope so. Apparently they were baseball fans and it was the couple's prize possession, yaddah, yaddah," Mark said.

"That would make sense."

"Well, now it's a bloody mess is what it is. I don't envy whoever has to clean it up when this is all over."

Jeremiah had cleaned up worse than that in his day, but refrained from saying so.

"It's good to have an open and shut case. Well, not good. People are dead, still. The kid's traumatized. So is his sister. She doesn't want to admit that her brother did this."

"Do you?" Jeremiah asked.

Mark looked at him sharply. "What do you mean?"

"You keep saying the case is so straightforward, like you're trying to convince yourself."

Mark blinked at him.

"Sorry, I know you're tired, stressed about Liam, you're just talking out loud," Jeremiah said.

"What if he didn't kill his parents?" Mark asked.

"Did he say he did?"

"He hasn't said anything yet. Just kept cradling that bat. The doctor had a devil of a time getting him to let go of it before they took them both to the police station."

"Why aren't you at the police station?"

"I'm not sure he's going to say anything meaningful for

a while. And, if he does, there's dozens of cops right there ready to witness it. I'll go in after I check on Liam and see how things are going, write up my notes, get ready to have the kid formally charged."

"What happens with a case like his?"

Mark shook his head. "That's for the district attorney and the doctors and his lawyer to figure out. Given the state he's in now I have a hard time seeing them being able to do anything but perhaps commit him to a mental institution for a couple of years. I don't know. Not my problem."

"No, it's not," Jeremiah said.

"Unless he didn't kill his parents. Kid like that has tantrums, both his sister and the doctor said so. Throws things sometimes."

"Okay," Jeremiah said.

The waitress dropped off their orders and Jeremiah picked up his fork and plunged it into his bowl of chicken fettuccine alfredo. Mark picked up his own fork but it hovered in the air above his spaghetti and meatballs without actually descending.

"So, I get it. He gets mad, frustrated, picks up the nearest thing he can find and throws it. Who hasn't thrown something at some point?" Mark mused.

"Probably a lot of people," Jeremiah said.

"Yeah, but, grab, throw, that's an impulse."

"It is."

"March into the other room, smash a case, grab a baseball bat, come back and bash your parents' heads in, one at a time, that takes more than a second. That takes fifteen, twenty seconds. More, maybe."

"It's certainly not throwing something either," Jeremiah pointed out.

"There was a 911 call placed. No talking, screaming, anything, just silence from what I understand."

"Your point?"

"You see your kid coming at you with a baseball bat and have enough time to pick up a phone you also have enough time to, I don't know, run, fight back, raise your arm to block the blow."

"I take it none of those things happened?"

Mark shook his head. "Not a one."

"That makes no sense."

"Unless neither of them were the one who placed the call."

"The kid?"

"On the floor rocking and moaning. I don't think he had the capacity at that point to dial the phone. Even if he had I think they could have heard him moaning or something."

Jeremiah cleared his throat. "Sounds like you've got a problem."

Mark swore. "I've got a big problem."

"The kid's not your killer."

Mark swore again.

~

Cindy was out of patience. It was well after lunchtime and she was on her sixth revision of the stupid memo. She was about to start screaming. It didn't matter who wrote a line, her or Mr. Cartwright. As soon as it was in black-and-white he hated it. She had no idea at this rate how either of them would accomplish anything ever. She couldn't believe that one single page memo a day was an acceptable output for either of their job descriptions.

Just breathe, she told herself as she stood, waiting for him to drop the axe on the latest version. He seemingly read it over three times. He picked up a pen on his desk and put it down half a dozen times. Finally he handed it back to her and glanced at his watch.

"I have to leave now for a luncheon. I won't be back today so this will have to do."

"Okay," she said, forcing herself not to give a shout of joy that it was over and that he was leaving for the day.

"Make copies and distribute them in all the mailboxes downstairs," he said as he stood up.

"Where are the mail-"

"Downstairs. They're impossible to miss," he said in an irritated tone. "Make sure you do that immediately. They need to see these memos as soon as possible."

"I'll do them right after my lunch break," she said.

"Now," he barked.

She wanted to punch him in the nose. For the life of her she could never remember wanting to hit another human being as badly as she wanted to hit him. Not even Kyle.

I think I have a new face for my dartboard at home, she told herself. She felt a smirk creeping over her face and she turned quickly to hide it.

She took the paper and found the copy machine. Once there she realized she had no idea how many copies she needed to make. She dropped the memo off on her desk and turned to Leo who had been back from his lunch break for a while.

"Do you know how many mailboxes are downstairs?" she asked.

He frowned. "No. I didn't know we had mailboxes downstairs."

"Oh good, so then you can tell me where to find them," she said.

He shook his head. "I don't envy you. Good luck."

"Thanks."

She headed for the elevator and made it down to the first floor. Once there she stayed close to the wall to avoid being run over by any equipment. She left the entrance alcove which didn't have anything more than the elevator and a time clock and entered the main floor. All around were shelving units and crates and forklifts moving in seemingly random patterns across the floor. She hugged the wall and began to work her way clockwise, hoping to run into someone she could ask about the mailboxes.

Finally a man in a hardhat with the name Bob on his nametag walked by.

"Excuse me!" she shouted to make herself heard.

He turned and looked at her.

"Hi, I'm new. Could you tell me where the mailboxes are?" she asked.

He jabbed a thumb over his shoulder and then kept walking. Well, at least she was going in the right direction. She kept walking until she made it to the corner of the building. There she found another alcove, this one had doors that led into two offices and a wall with what looked like nearly a hundred mailboxes on it.

She resisted the urge to check and see if Leo's name was on one of them. If so, it would certainly be a surprise to him.

She counted and discovered that there were actually 108 mailboxes, although ten of them had no names on them. Presumably they didn't belong to anyone so she had no need to put the memo in those. That left 98 copies to make.

Armed with that knowledge she turned and traced her way back to the elevator.

Twenty minutes later Cindy was back at her desk. She'd made the copies, hastily stuffed one in each mailbox and made it back upstairs. She glanced at the clock and saw that it was after two.

What a waste of most of a workday, she thought to herself.

The good news was that after her lunch she'd have less than two hours left in the hateful place. At least, for the day. She was not looking forward to coming back the next morning, particularly since her boss would be in.

She hadn't brought a lunch with her and she hadn't noticed any obvious places to grab a quick bite as she drove there this morning. She'd planned on figuring out where her coworkers were heading and following them to lunch. She stood up and looked over the wall at Leo.

"Where is a good place close by to get something to eat?" she asked him.

"Glad you're finally getting to take a break," he said.

"Tell me about it."

"There's a burger place across the street and down half a block."

"It's good?"

"I didn't say that," he said, curling his lip. "Down on the second floor there's a lunchroom. There's some soups and things like that in a vending machine."

It was her turn to curl up her lip.

"I know. I tend to bring my own."

"Fun," she said.

Lately getting away from work for an hour was usually the highlight of her day.

"Do you have to get grilled by the guard going and coming?"

He nodded. "Even if you walk. It's one of the perks of working here."

"Vending machine it is," she said with a sigh.

"When you get off the elevator turn right and then take another right."

"Thanks."

Cindy took the elevator down to the second floor. She was a bit relieved that when the doors opened it looked like a normal office building and not another warehouse type floor. She turned right and came to a hallway where she took another right. At the far end of it she could see an open door and glimpse a table and some chairs through it.

Encouraged that she was heading to the right place she picked up the pace. As unappetizing as vending machine soup sounded, she was getting really hungry and was ready to eat just about anything.

As she neared the room she could hear someone talking. There were pauses, but whoever they were talking to she could only hear the one voice. Just as she was about to cross the threshold into the room she heard something that made her freeze in her tracks.

"I'm telling you. Rose just disappeared."

8

"Why can't anything ever be simple?" Mark asked with a sigh.

"You really don't want me to answer that," Jeremiah said with a smirk.

"Thanks," Mark said sarcastically. "Man, this day just keeps getting better and better. Liam picked a helluva day to get the crap kicked out of him."

Jeremiah raised an eyebrow but didn't say anything.

"So, how do two people get their heads caved in without trying to get away or defend themselves?"

"Sounds like their killer took them by surprise," Jeremiah said.

"And I'd like to know how they were caught completely off guard if they'd just heard the glass case break. If anything you think they would have headed in there to see what happened."

"Maybe they were heading in there and they started in another part of the house," Jeremiah suggested.

"No, I don't think they were facing the dining room. If they were, they would have seen it coming. And the blows were to the backs of their heads."

"So, they didn't hear the glass case break," Jeremiah said.

"Meaning it happened earlier. The killer was probably waiting for them."

"Expensive murder weapon."

"You're right," Mark said. "Unless, the killer wasn't intending to kill them."

"You mean, they caught him or her by surprise?"

"Exactly. Heck, maybe it was a robbery gone wrong. Killer grabs the bat. Before he can make his getaway he hears them in the kitchen. He sneaks in, kills them in a panic, then drops the bat, also in a panic, and runs."

"It could happen. How do you explain the 911 call, though?"

"Maybe he was hiding in some other part of the house when they came home and discovered the bat missing."

"And the call center doesn't pick up the sound of the caller being hit or falling to the floor?" Jeremiah asked.

Mark winced. "I don't know. But, I need to find out if they'd left the house this morning or not," Mark said, reaching for his phone.

~

Cindy forced herself to step into the lunchroom. Once across the threshold her eyes locked onto the sole other occupant, a man with sandy colored hair a couple of years younger than her with his sleeves rolled up to his elbows and his tie askew. He was on his cell phone and turned to look at her.

She forced herself to smile at him. She turned and walked toward the vending machines against the wall.

"I've got to go, we'll talk later," he said.

He ended his call and then scurried from the room before she could say anything to him.

Curiosity was burning within her. Was he talking about

the Rose who used to sit at her desk? Whoever it was he seemed concerned about them and the fact that they'd vanished. Her mind raced, wondering if it was the same woman. It seemed likely to her, but she tried to tell herself she was jumping to conclusions. The only mystery here was what she was going to find in these vending machines that was even remotely edible.

Her eyes drifted to the machine with the chips and candy bars and she forced her attention back to the one with the soups. At least they were microwave soups of recognizable brands, so less suspect than she'd feared. She finally chose a cup of ramen. She added water from the sink at the other end of the room and then popped it into the microwave.

She sat down with it at a table a couple minutes later. She pulled out her phone. There were no messages from Jeremiah, which was a bit surprising. Maybe his day had been hectic, too.

She called him and he picked up just before it went to voicemail.

"Hi," he said. "I was wondering when you would be calling."

"I'm just now getting lunch," she said. "It's been an...interesting...day so far."

She longed to tell him more, but figured it was better not to complain about her new boss while actually at work. "I'll tell you all about it later. How is your day going?"

"Well, it's been a bit rough. Liam was attacked. He's in the hospital."

"Oh my gosh! Is he okay?"

"The next forty-eight hours will tell. He's got a lot of broken bones, but they think they stopped the internal bleeding."

She sat there, stunned. "Is Mark okay?"

"Yeah, he's shaken up, but fine. We're having lunch before heading back to the hospital. He wasn't with Liam this morning when it happened."

"Do they know who did it?"

"Not yet. There's a lot to tell, but I've got to get moving here soon."

"Yes, of course. Well, I'll come to the hospital after work."

"Okay, see you soon. Love you."

"Love you, too," she said.

Despite everything just hearing him say those words gave her a happy glow. She was convinced that she was never going to get used to hearing him say it.

They ended the call and she turned her attention to her ramen even as her mind raced ahead thinking and worrying about Liam. The last thing Mark needed was to lose another partner. Besides, she really liked Liam. He was a good guy.

"It seems like everything's in chaos these days," she muttered to herself.

She had an entire hour for lunch, but she was done eating in fifteen minutes. She wished she could go back to her desk and just leave early instead. She was going to need to start bringing a book or something with her. She finally stood up. She might as well get back to her desk and start cleaning it out. Maybe if she was lucky she could get it all done by the end of the day.

Jeremiah was tired. The adrenaline of the morning was

wearing off and with nothing to actively do, no one to pursue, he could really feel the drain.

"You okay?" Mark asked as they walked into the hospital.

"Long day," he said. It was true enough. It just felt like an endless, useless day of waiting and reporting to others.

"Tell me about it," Mark muttered.

Once inside the hospital a nurse was able to direct them to Liam's room. As soon as he had the room number Jeremiah called and gave it to Rebecca who vowed she would be there soon if she had to move mountains. Or, in her case, policemen. He hung up with her just as they entered Liam's room.

He had prepared himself so he was not shocked to see just how bad Liam looked. The man's face was swollen with cuts and bruises on it. His arm was in a cast and there was bruising visible above that. He lay very still with several machines hooked up to him and an IV drip going.

Next to him Mark made a little sound of dismay and moved forward quickly. "Hey, partner, we're here," he said, his voice cracking slightly.

Liam's eyelids fluttered and then slowly opened. He stared from Mark to Jeremiah and back again. Slowly his lips began to move, but no sound came out. He licked his lips and tried again.

"What happened?"

"We were hoping you could tell us," Mark said, the anxiety clear in his voice.

Jeremiah stepped forward. "You're in the hospital. You're going to be okay. Someone attacked you early this morning while you were walking to Rebecca's shop."

Liam's eyes opened wider and Jeremiah hastened to

add, "Don't worry, Rebecca's fine. She'll be here shortly."

"Okay," Liam said.

"Did you see who hit you?" Mark asked.

"I didn't even know I was hit," Liam said slowly.

"Do you remember walking toward Rebecca's shop?" Jeremiah asked.

"Yes."

"Did you have flowers with you? Yellow roses by any chance?"

"Yes, how did you know?" Liam asked.

"There were a couple of petals on the ground next to where you were found," Jeremiah said.

Mark glanced at him. Jeremiah had no idea if the officers on scene had taken note of the petals as being significant. Hopefully they had. Liam's attacker had likely been the one to take the flowers. The question was, why would he bother? If he was looking for a trophy or proof of the attack he would have taken something else, something more personal.

"Did you see a motorcycle parked near the shop?" Jeremiah asked.

"Yes."

"Did you see the rider?"

"No."

As soon as Rebecca got there he'd ask her about the motorcycle. If it was indeed gone before she made it onto the scene then he was certain whoever the rider was attacked Liam.

"Care to share?" Mark asked with a raised eyebrow.

"In a little while," Jeremiah said.

Liam was in obvious, understandable distress. The faster they could get past this and let him rest the better.

"Have you received any threats of any kind recently?" Jeremiah asked.

"No."

"Has anyone you helped put away been recently paroled or have the ability and desire to reach out beyond prison to do this?"

Mark squirmed and Jeremiah realized he was just now realizing that he could be in danger as well. His discomfort couldn't be helped at this point. Either he was in danger or he wasn't and the sooner they figured that out, too, the better for all concerned.

Liam glanced at Mark and frowned slightly. "I don't know...Mark?"

"I don't know either, but we'll find out as soon as possible," Mark said.

The detective's phone rang and he scrambled to retrieve it. "It's the car place," he muttered and then stepped outside to take the call. He was back just moments later. "It's ready," he said gruffly.

"I was supposed to pick you up this morning, I'm so sorry," Liam said.

"Don't worry about it. I made other arrangements," Mark told him.

"I'll take you to pick it up after Rebecca gets here," Jeremiah said.

"Thanks. Then I've got to get to the station."

"You don't have to stay," Liam said.

"Stop it," Mark said roughly. "Of course we're staying."

One look at Mark's face told Jeremiah that the detective was nervous about leaving his partner alone when the threat against him was out there somewhere. Jeremiah felt the same way.

~

Mark's head was spinning. Jeremiah's suggestion that whoever had done this to Liam might be someone that he'd helped put away wasn't sitting well with him. It was always a danger, but the beating Liam had taken was horrible. Retaliation against Pine Springs police officers was virtually unheard of. This wasn't Los Angeles. They didn't have many violent criminals they put away. No gang members for certain. The killers they did put away for the most part weren't hardened criminals, just people who had snapped and decided to take the law into their own hands.

There were exceptions, of course, but the thought that this was past work related really rattled him. If this was retaliation against Liam then he could very well be in the crosshairs, too. He needed to get some answers and fast, ideally before he talked to Traci. She'd be asking these same questions and not in a polite way. She turned into a lioness these days if she perceived any threat to her family, no matter how remote or unrealistic.

He closed his eyes and grimaced. He couldn't wait until he had answers to call Traci. He'd promised himself he'd call and tell her as soon as he knew what Liam's condition was. Well, he had answers about that now, at least, for the moment barring complications.

"If you need to call Traci, do it," Jeremiah said suddenly.

Mark looked at him sharply. "How did you know that's what I was thinking about?"

"You were fidgeting with your wedding ring. I figured

you were thinking about her. You were exhibiting signs of anxiety therefore thinking about calling and telling her what happened to Liam."

"Just join the police force already if you're going to scrutinize people like that," Mark snapped.

Jeremiah raised an eyebrow. "I've got a job. Don't need another one."

"I'm sorry," Mark said with a sigh. He turned to Liam. "I'll be back in a minute. I'm just going to go call Traci and let her know you're okay," he said with forced cheerfulness.

"Tell her hi," Liam said.

Mark nodded and left the room. He realized he was starting to sweat. This whole thing was making him uneasy. He kept telling himself that Liam was going to be just fine. He was awake, talking, he'd be up and walking in no time.

I can't lose another partner, he thought as he found a quiet corner to call Traci from.

She picked up right away and she sounded tired, too. "Hey."

"Hey, how are you doing?"

"What's wrong?" she asked, clearly hearing the trepidation in his voice.

"I found out why Liam didn't come to pick me up this morning," he said.

"Oh?"

"Someone jumped him near Rebecca's shop and beat him up. He's in the hospital."

"What?!"

"Yes. The doctors need to keep him for observation. He's got some broken ribs, a broken arm."

"What are the doctors observing, exactly?" she asked.

"He had some internal bleeding," Mark said, wincing as the words came out. "They're watching his spleen and his liver."

It was a testament to how tired and upset Traci was that she swore. Usually she left that to him. After a few seconds he could hear her taking a deep breath, clearly trying to calm herself down.

"Who did it?" she finally asked.

"We don't know."

"You mean this psychopath is out there?" she demanded, her voice raised until she was nearly shouting.

"We're going to find him," Mark said.

"Is it someone looking for revenge?" she asked quickly.

Mark sighed. "We have no evidence that it was work-related in any way. Maybe it was random, or maybe..."

"Maybe what?" she asked when he didn't finish.

"Maybe it has something to do with his past, his family. Even Jeremiah's noticed that he doesn't talk a lot about them."

There was a pause and then she said, "That doesn't seem as likely as the other."

"Are you sure? Because, whoever did this, it seemed very personal. They really beat the crap out of him. It's amazing he wasn't killed," he said, voice getting shakier as he went.

He hadn't meant to tell her that. He wasn't doing anything to allay her fears. He was only aggravating them for both her and himself.

"You honestly think this is some specter from his past and not some criminal he's crossed paths with as a cop? Or some guy that just has a problem with cops in general? It's not like there haven't been a lot of hate crimes across the country lately."

"It's not random, it's personal," Mark snapped.

"What makes you so certain? Maybe someone found the nearest cop and took out their rage on him."

"No, this was a planned attack, there was a reason behind it," he said forcefully.

He realized that he had no evidence to back up that theory. He just couldn't bring himself to think it was random. No, he was convinced this had something to do with Liam personally.

He realized that Traci had grown silent.

"Are you still there?" he asked, regretting the tone he'd taken.

"You know what your problem is?" Traci asked.

"What?"

"You're afraid of losing another partner and the whole thing being a mystery, just like Paul."

"I think there's more going on than that," Mark said slowly.

"There always is with you, but face it, you're freaking out because Liam's not out of the woods and you have no idea who attacked him or what's going on."

"Alright, say I am having some sort of flashback to losing Paul and discovering I never even knew Paul. Say that this is something from Liam's past coming back to try and take him away. What do you suggest I do about it?"

"I suggest you solve the mystery."

"Thanks, Hon," he said, unable to keep the sarcasm out of his voice. "Because I wasn't planning on using the full resources of the police department to figure out who did this to Liam and lock him away forever."

"No, idiot," she said, matching his sarcasm. "Not that mystery."

"What do you mean?" he asked sharply.

"You've had what might be the final pieces to the riddle that is Paul in your possession for weeks now and you haven't done anything about it. I think you're afraid to close the case."

A chill danced up Mark's spine and he felt something cold slither in his stomach.

"What are you saying?"

"I'm saying, you need to finish the Paul mystery once and for all before it kills you."

9

Cindy found a box containing packages of paper by the copy machine. Since there was only one package remaining in it she was able to put the paper in the machine and free up the box. She took it back to her cubicle and sat down, ready to tackle all of Rose's personal things that had been left behind. Glancing uneasily at the desk she couldn't help but think she also might need a trash bag. She had a tiny trash can at her desk that seemed like it would be woefully inadequate to the task at hand.

She started by grabbing a pink sweater off the desk. She used it to wrap the glass votive pen holder in and put them and the flower pens carefully in the box. The stuffed unicorn followed. She took the rose pendant off the monitor and found an envelope she could seal it in so it wouldn't get tangled or overlooked. She put in the red stapler. It seemed pretty clear it had belonged to Rose given the rhinestone encrusted name on it. Whether or not it had started out that way, it was certainly hers now.

Pinned to the low walls of the cubicle were all kinds of pictures of cats and unicorns. She carefully removed all of them, dumped the pins in the shallow desk drawer where they belonged and put the pictures in the box. A small ceramic unicorn sitting underneath the monitor was the next to go after she found a purple scarf wadded up in a pile of papers, the edge of it just barely sticking out. She wrapped the unicorn in the scarf and deposited them both in the box.

A small cube of motivational saying sticky notes went next. Those were definitely not company issue. They had cats on them with cute little sayings. Cindy couldn't help but like them and wonder where Rose had bought them. She could definitely see how something like that could cheer up the drab little work station.

Why would she leave all these things behind? the thought came to her again.

It made no sense. Even if she had decided to abandon the work related items, why leave behind clothing and the necklace? It just felt wrong somehow. Then there was the picture of her and the older woman who could be her grandmother.

Cindy picked it up. She didn't know why she hadn't put the picture in its heart themed frame into the box yet. Something about it was just odd to her. She took a closer look at the frame.

It was silver, with hearts carved into it. At the bottom the words True Love were inscribed. It was very romantic, not the kind of frame one usually used for a picture with their grandmother. It looked like something you'd use to frame a picture of your sweetheart.

She started to put the frame in the box, but her hand hesitated. It was like she couldn't let go of the frame. She put it back on the desk and looked at it more closely. She turned it around and discovered that the picture just slipped in the top. You didn't have to take the back off. She grasped the edge of the picture and gently pulled up on it. She took it out then turned the frame back around.

There was another picture in the frame. It had been

behind the picture of Rose and her grandmother. This picture also had Rose in it. She was wearing a little black dress and sitting on the knee of a man dressed up like Santa Claus. She was blushing and half-turned away from the camera to look at the man in the suit. Her skin was glowing, her eyes were soft, pupils dilated.

It was the kind of picture that fit in the frame for a very specific reason. Rose looked like a woman in love.

~

When Rebecca finally walked into the hospital room and laid eyes on Liam Jeremiah couldn't help but think that she looked like a woman in love. She rushed over to him and grabbed his good hand and kissed it.

"Are you okay?" she asked, voice trembling.

"I am now," Liam said softly.

Jeremiah smiled. From the way that Liam was looking at Rebecca it was clear how this was all going to play out. He was obviously in love with her.

Good for them, he thought.

With his next breath, though, he prayed for their safety and that Liam would pull through everything alright.

As though sensing his thoughts on their behalf Rebecca turned quickly to look at him. "Thank you, for everything," she said.

He nodded and stood. "You're welcome. I need to drive Mark to pick up his car. I figure we'll do that now."

"See you later," Liam said.

"I'll walk you out," Rebecca said hastily.

"There's no need," Mark said.

"I'll just be a minute," she told Liam, ignoring Mark.

She had something she wanted to discuss. Jeremiah stepped outside with Mark, but then stopped before they made it to the lobby.

"I think someone should be with him round the clock," he said quietly. "Until whoever did this is found."

"I'll arrange for officers to watch him," Mark said.

"Thank you, both," Rebecca said, turning paler.

"What happened at your shop?" Jeremiah asked.

She dropped her eyes. "Things had been moved around, but it doesn't seem like anything was stolen."

"That's odd," Jeremiah said.

She shrugged.

There was more to it than that. She was holding something back. Jeremiah was about to press her when Mark reached out and touched his arm.

"We should get going. I'll touch base with the officers on the scene, see what they found."

Jeremiah nodded slowly, but kept his eyes on Rebecca, willing her to look up at him. She didn't. Her eyes still on the ground, she mumbled, "I'll see you later."

She turned and disappeared inside Liam's room.

Mark headed for the parking lot and Jeremiah followed reluctantly. Once they were in the car he turned to the detective. "She's hiding something."

"Everyone hides something," Mark said absently.

"I mean, about her shop. I think there was more to what happened there than someone rifling through her stuff."

"Maybe and maybe she's just too stressed out to focus on anything but Liam at the moment," Mark said.

"I don't know, I think-"

"Do you think he's going to die?" Mark blurted out suddenly.

Jeremiah blinked in surprise at the sudden shift in conversation.

"I think he's strong, and he's got the best care possible with doctors and nurses who will be watching him like a hawk."

"That doesn't answer my question."

Jeremiah hesitated. He'd seen men die from a lot less. He'd also seen men survive a lot worse. "He wants to live. That's one of the most important factors. And it looks like he has someone to live for. I think he'll pull through."

"Okay."

"What's wrong?"

"My partner's in the hospital and he could still die and I hate waiting to figure out if he's truly going to be okay," Mark snapped.

"And, just like Rebecca, you're not saying the whole truth."

Mark slammed his fist into the dashboard.

The violent outburst was uncharacteristic of him. Jeremiah waited a few seconds and then said, "I don't think the car is the source of your problems."

"I can't lose another partner," Mark said, his voice tight.

Jeremiah had suspected as much. Paul had been taken in sudden, horrific fashion in a way that couldn't have been anticipated by Mark, not really. The same could end up being true for Liam.

"You won't," Jeremiah said. It might be a lie, but hopefully not. Even if it was, it was the lie the other man needed to hear to get through the moment.

"Partners are supposed to be there for each other, have each other's backs. I wanted to be there for him. I should have been there for him. How can I be, though, when he keeps me in the dark and doesn't tell me everything?"

"I don't think he's intentionally kept you in the dark. I mean, there are things people don't like to talk about, and what happened to him may or may not have any connection to that. Either way, though, you'll find the man who did this," Jeremiah said reassuringly.

Mark was silent for a long minute. Then he said, "What happened to him, I don't understand. It makes no sense."

Jeremiah glanced at Mark who was staring fixedly out the window. He had the look of a man haunted by something. Jeremiah had seen that look in men's eyes before. Usually before they did something stupid.

Jeremiah hesitated for a moment. "Are we still talking about Liam?"

Mark punched the dashboard again.

~

Cindy stared at the photo of Rose and Santa Claus. She shifted her attention from the young woman in the photo to the man in the Santa Claus suit. She wondered who he was. The fake beard covered most of his face and his hat was pulled down low on his forehead. All that she could really make out were the eyes, and there was nothing truly remarkable about them. They looked brown in color.

She pulled the photo out and turned it over to look at the back, wondering if there was anything written on it. There wasn't, as it turned out.

She put the photo back and then put the picture of Rose and her grandmother over it. Why had she chosen to cover the first photo? If she and the man in it had been dating and broken up wouldn't she have gotten rid of the photo instead of just hiding it? Cindy put the frame in the box. Whatever the mystery there, it was not hers to solve.

After she'd done that there were still a lot of things on the desk, but they all seemed work related. With a sigh she opened the large, bottom drawer that was crammed full of stuff. She pulled out the top stack of papers, wondering what kind of filing system, if any, Rose had used.

She dropped the papers on the desk and discovered that underneath there was yet another sweater. Rose apparently had a habit of leaving clothes at work. She dumped it in the box as well. Below it she discovered a tin box and she pulled it up onto the desk and opened the lid.

There were an assortment of things in the tin. There were some cardboard drink coasters bearing the logos of various restaurants and bars. There was an oyster shell, a flyer for an upcoming tour of Phantom of the Opera which would be opening in Los Angeles on Friday, and a pen with the name of a hotel in Los Angeles.

She looked at the flyer with interest. She wondered if Joseph and Geanie were going, given their love for Phantom of the Opera. She'd have to ask them since Geanie hadn't mentioned anything about it yet.

She turned the flyer over and on the back it said G34, G36. Seat numbers maybe? Little hearts had been hand drawn around them.

She dropped the flyer back in the box and picked up an envelope. There was a handwritten note inside.

Rose,
    Thank you for organizing the amazing
Christmas party. You are a treasure. I don't
know what the company would ever do

without you. And I still don't know how you managed to talk him into being Santa Claus! Truly a woman of astonishing talents!! Thank you again. From all of us.
Always yours,
- Beau

She read the note a second time. Christmas again. And whoever Beau was, he clearly knew who the man in the Santa suit was. She couldn't help but wonder if Beau always signed his letters *Always yours* or if he really liked Rose. She shook her head. *Office drama.* The last thing she needed to do was get sucked into it.

She folded the letter and put it back in the envelope. Clearly this was a box of mementos that Rose was holding onto. She only half-heartedly looked through the rest just to make sure that nothing else had gotten mixed in. It didn't seem to.

She put the lid back on the tin and added it to the box which was close to full. She rifled through the rest of the things in the bottom drawer and found three letters from an insurance company addressed to Rose. They seemed to deal with her health insurance and so she dumped them in the box as well.

She moved the box up onto the desk behind her. She then returned her attention to the drawers. Everything else in the bottom one seemed strictly work related, so she closed it. She had just opened the drawer above it when she suddenly had a sense that someone was behind her.

She spun around and stared up at the face of the guy she'd seen earlier in the lunchroom. His features were contorted in rage. In his hand was the red stapler from the box. He was gripping it so tightly that his knuckles had turned white.

He opened his mouth in a snarl. "Where is she?"

10

"Excuse me?" Cindy asked, shaken.

She glanced over and noticed that Leo wasn't at his desk. She forced herself to her feet and took a couple of swift steps to put distance between herself and the man glaring at her.

"You heard me. Where is Rose?" he asked, waving the stapler threateningly in his fist.

"I don't know," she said. "I'm a temp. I just got here today."

"What are you doing with her things?" he asked, getting red in the face.

"I was told to box them up," she said, taking another step back and eyeing the stapler warily.

"Why? Where has she gone?"

"How should I know?" she snapped, still freaked out.

She took another step backward and ran into the wall of another cubicle. She felt trapped and she glanced around for a way out or a weapon she could use to defend herself.

He stood there, fuming, the fist holding the stapler shaking. Then, suddenly, he seemed to slump over and it was as though all the fight left him.

"I just want to know how to find her," he said, so softly she almost didn't hear him.

"You should ask Mr. Cartwright. He's the one who's going to be mailing the box," Cindy said, dropping her defenses slightly.

The man looked beaten, weary, and her heart suddenly went out to him. As much as she just wanted to get away from him she was surprised to hear herself ask, "Are you okay?"

His features suddenly crumpled. He collapsed into her chair and stared idly at the desk for a moment.

"We're friends. At least, I thought we were. She didn't tell me she was quitting. I don't think she told anyone. I don't know how to get hold of her outside work."

"How do you know she quit?" Cindy asked.

He looked up sharply. "What do you mean?"

"How do you know she wasn't fired?"

He shook his head. "They make a big deal about that kind of thing around here. If she'd been fired the whole building would have known."

Cindy thought about the fence and the security guard in the parking lot. What he said didn't surprise her. This seemed like the kind of place that would take security very seriously.

"She was here last Friday. I walked her to her car and she said she'd see me Monday. Yesterday she never showed up and now you're here."

"Maybe she called in and quit," Cindy suggested.

"What could have happened over the weekend to make that happen?" he asked.

"I don't know. Maybe she got another job offer or had a parent fall ill in another state. Maybe she eloped, who knows," she said, starting to grasp at straws.

He jerked when she suggested the last possibility.

He had a crush on Rose, she realized.

"Are you Beau by any chance?" she asked.

"Yes, how did you know?" he asked.

"I was told to clean out the desk and I've been trying to sort the business papers from the personal ones. I found a note you sent her."

"What did it say?" he asked, face turning suddenly pale.

"A thank you for a Christmas party was all," she said, again regarding him with suspicion.

"Oh, that," he said.

She paused. The whole situation was weird. Maybe years of stumbling into mysteries was making her paranoid. Maybe there really was more here than met the eye. She cleared her throat. "What do you think happened to Rose?"

He stood up abruptly and made as if to go. He was several feet away before he turned and looked back. His eyes were haunted. "Nothing good," he whispered.

~

Mark picked up his car at the shop and headed back to the police station. He had thanked Jeremiah briefly for driving him all over and the rabbi had told him not to worry about it. Still, he was glad to be away from the man and his questions. He was sick to death of questions for the day.

Unfortunately nothing but questions waited for him back at the station. When he pulled into the parking lot he briefly considered driving right back out again. If he left, though, he'd head home and questions waited for him there, too.

He sighed and pulled into a parking space. The ones that awaited him here might be easier to answer. Moments like this he wished he could actually pray to some higher power for strength or patience or whatever it was people prayed for.

He got out of the car and marched into the station. He made it to his desk and picked up the stack of messages that were on it. At that moment he felt the loss of a partner even more keenly. Panic knifed through him and he forced himself to take several deep, slow breaths.

This is all doable. I've been without a partner before. I can do it again. Besides, it's just for a few days, he told himself.

Maybe he could talk Traci into trying to get Geanie and Joseph to take the twins overnight so he could get some decent sleep. Maybe take them for a couple of nights.

He shook himself hard and dropped the messages on his desk. He went and found one of the officers who had been at the crime scene earlier. The man told him that Officer Taylor had gone home for the day. Mark was glad that he had. Hopefully he'd calm down once he'd had a chance to get some distance from the events. He also told Mark that Casey was in an interrogation room with his doctor and an attorney who had just arrived.

Mark headed over to the interrogation room and winced. It was the same one he'd been busy torturing a guy in while Paul was off being killed. He took another deep breath trying to calm the new burst of panic that threatened to tear him apart.

Get a grip on yourself, he ordered.

He turned around and went to the kitchen area. He made himself a cup of coffee and made a cup of hot chocolate as well. He'd read somewhere that chocolate could help calm a person down. Why he never remembered that when Traci was in a cranky mood he didn't for the life of him know.

He walked back over to the interrogation room and sat down at the table across from the others. Casey was sitting, his eyes fixed on the table. The lawyer was sitting on one side of Casey and the doctor was sitting on the other side. He addressed the latter, "I appreciate you taking time out of your busy schedule to stay here with us."

The man nodded, but didn't say anything.

"I brought Casey some hot chocolate, is that okay?" he asked.

Casey looked up at that and began nodding at the same time the doctor did.

"Here you go," Mark said, smiling and pushing the Styrofoam cup across the table to him.

"Coffee?" he asked the doctor, lifting the second cup.

"Yes, please," the man said.

Mark handed it to him. As much as he wanted coffee at that moment he was also pretty sure the caffeine would just give him the jitters right then. Which would be bad.

The lawyer, an older woman with her grey hair pulled into a severe bun, leaned forward. "I represent the family and we are interested in getting this over with in the least stressful way. To that end we are prepared to make a deal. Casey will make a formal confession in exchange for confinement in a... hospital... with visitation rights from his sister."

Mark held up a hand and cut her off. "I appreciate that you are trying to make this as painless as possible. However, I believe you're jumping the gun here."

"In what way?" the lawyer asked, narrowing her eyes at him.

Mark took a deep breath. "I'm not convinced that Casey here is our man."

"What are you talking about?" the lawyer demanded, eyes narrowing even further.

"Despite appearances, I don't think Casey did it. We are going to be expanding our investigation to try and locate other suspects."

"What other evidence do you need?" the lawyer demanded.

Mark stared at her intently and he noticed that the doctor looked as surprised as he felt.

"Why are you so intent to close the book on this?" he asked.

"Because, obviously, the longer this gets drawn out the harder it is on everyone in the family"

"On Casey and Ruth you mean?"

She nodded.

"And how much harder will a wrongful imprisonment be on them both?" Mark challenged. "Isn't them being together worth fighting for?"

"Yes," the doctor said.

"Thank you, Doctor," Mark said. "You told me earlier that you were convinced that Casey wasn't capable of...what happened this morning."

"And I stand by that," the man said.

"So, why are you the one person in the room not on Casey's side?" Mark asked the lawyer pointedly.

"I am not the one who needs to be answering questions," she said tartly.

"Perhaps you should be," Mark snapped. "You are the family's lawyer?"

"I am," she bristled.

"How long?"

"The last few years."

"So, you had a relationship with the deceased. Can you account for your whereabouts this morning?"

"Why you, son of a-"

"Language, counselor," Mark interrupted with a smirk. It wasn't often he rattled an attorney like he had just rattled this one. He was surprised at her attitude, though. It only served to further convince him that everything wasn't what it appeared.

"We are done here," the woman said, shoving her notepad into her briefcase.

"One of us is, at least," he said, unable to keep himself from goading her more.

He glanced at Casey and hesitated. There was the question of what to do with the young man for the moment. Before he could express his thoughts the doctor spoke up.

"If you release Casey into his sister's custody I can arrange for a nurse to come and stay with them for the next few days while everything gets sorted out," he said.

"That would be my first choice," Mark admitted even as the lawyer stormed from the room.

"I'll call her and arrange it," he said. He hesitated a moment then asked, "What do you have to do on your end?"

"I'll put in a call to Protective Services just to be on the safe side. They shouldn't have a problem releasing Casey into his sister's custody especially for the next few days while everyone figures out what to do next. As far as the department, there's nothing to do since there were never any charges brought against Casey today," Mark said. "He's free to go as soon as I can make that call and his sister can come and pick him up."

"Wonderful. If it's okay I'd like to stay until then, help

keep him calm."

"Your help in that would be greatly appreciated," Mark told him. "I'll be back in a few minutes."

Casey just kept his eyes down on the table. Mark had no idea how much the young man had heard of what they'd been saying, if anything. He wasn't rocking and moaning like he had been in the house, but something about his posture made him seem even farther away than he had been then.

I'll have to ask Cindy and Jeremiah to say a prayer for him, he thought as he left the room.

~

After Jeremiah had dropped Mark off at the mechanic he had driven back to the synagogue. The day was nearly over and he struggled with a desire to return to the hospital and question Rebecca more about what she and the police officers had discovered in her shop.

He kept telling himself it wasn't his job and if he asked at this point it would just be prying. He countered his own arguments by telling himself that all the prying and meddling in the world was worth it if it helped out his friends, particularly Mark.

He kept praying for Liam and for Mark. The former to be alright and the latter to let go of the pain and fear he was carrying. The past could creep up on a person and haunt them in unexpected ways. That was clearly happening to Mark. Liam was a completely different person than Paul and his situation was also different. Mark, though, wasn't seeing the differences but only the similarities such as they were.

When Jeremiah pulled into the parking lot at the synagogue he glanced over at the church parking lot from long habit and felt the familiar sinking feeling when he didn't see Cindy's car.

I hate this, he thought to himself as he parked and slowly got out of his car. He was close to the hedge that separated the two parking lots. As he started walking toward his office a man emerged from the church and waved at him.

Jeremiah waved back when he recognized the church's youth pastor, Dave "Wildman" Wyman. He expected to see the other man head to his car, but instead Dave changed direction and made a beeline for him. Jeremiah stopped, wondering what Wildman wanted from him.

He better not even think about asking me to chaperone an event or be a camp counselor again, Jeremiah thought. To date the other man hadn't, but Jeremiah still cringed inwardly whenever he saw him.

Wildman cut through a path in the hedge and came to a stop in front of him. "Hey, how's it going?" he asked.

It was an odd opener. They knew each other, but didn't tend to interact much beyond the passing wave.

"I'm tired of not sharing adjacent work places with Cindy," he said before he could stop himself.

Wildman nodded. "A lot of people at the church are unhappy and want her back."

"I'm betting the pastor isn't one of them," Jeremiah said, unable to hide his sarcasm.

Wildman grimaced, but didn't say anything.

Jeremiah took a deep breath. "What can I do for you?"

"I'd like to schedule an appointment to talk with you."

"Okay, about what?" Jeremiah asked, puzzled.

"I'd rather wait until we talk to tell you what about," Wildman said.

"Okay, should I be worried or intrigued?"

"Neither, both, I don't know," the youth pastor admitted, looking intensely uncomfortable.

"And now I'm both," Jeremiah said with what he hoped was a reassuring smile. Sometimes he could get that look just right and people seemed to relax. Other times, especially the last several months, he got it wrong and just set people further on edge.

He knew that was because he still hadn't gotten used to being just a civilian again. He himself was on edge more than he had been before. He didn't like that he wasn't as good at hiding it as he should be, but he had to remind himself that the man he was trying to be in this community, the rabbi, wouldn't be able to hide his emotions as well as the man he used to be.

"Is that okay?" Wildman asked hesitantly.

"That's fine, Dave. When would you like to meet?"

"Not this week, I'm slammed."

"We could meet after work."

"No! I mean, I'd prefer to do this during business hours."

"Is it business related?" Jeremiah asked, raising an eyebrow.

"No, it's not," the other man admitted.

"Okay, well, let me know when works for you and we can make it happen," Jeremiah said.

"Thanks, I appreciate that."

"Anytime."

The youth pastor reached out and quickly shook his hand before turning and hurrying to his car.

Okay, that was weird, Jeremiah thought as he watched the other man get in his vehicle and drive away.

It was like he was surrounded by weird at the moment. He glanced around, wondering if anyone else had seen the exchange. He wouldn't put it past the head pastor at the church to accuse him of trying to poach his staff, corrupt them in some way.

Wouldn't that be hilarious if Wildman wanted to convert to Judaism, he thought. He actually laughed out loud. He didn't know exactly why, but the thought amused him.

His phone rang and he pulled it out of his pocket. He frowned when he saw that Rebecca was calling on the phone he'd given her.

"Rebecca?" he asked as he answered.

There was a long pause on the other end and then he heard a low, raspy voice say, "No."

"Who is this?"

There was another long pause then the voice whispered again, "Get over here right now or else."

11

"Who is this?" Jeremiah demanded.

"No cops," the voice hissed. The call ended abruptly.

Jeremiah spun around and was back in his car and peeling out of the parking lot seconds later. He wanted to call Mark, to have him meet him at the hospital. The man on the other end of the line had been clear about that, though, and Jeremiah had to assume he had the ability to know if Jeremiah tried to bring some with him. Another time he might have chanced it, but the detective was too tired to be sneaky and subtle and try to make it to Liam's room without being found out.

He was about to call Cindy when he realized he couldn't do that to her. He couldn't panic her with time still left on her first day at the new job. He needed to know what this was before he brought in the others.

Above all, he was worrying about Liam and Rebecca. What had happened that someone else had the phone he'd given her? And if something was happening to her, who was watching Liam? He had no way of knowing if the police guard Mark had intended to establish had gone into effect yet.

There were days when he couldn't help but wonder why the universe wasn't content to leave him alone. Most people lived their lives without ever being involved in police investigations. How he managed to get swept up in so many of them was beyond comprehension. G-d had a strange sense of humor. That was all he could figure some days.

Then again, maybe it was his ability to spot trouble that was different. Perhaps many people encountered crimes, murders, even, and just walked on by because they didn't pay attention to what was going on around them.

It was a chilling thought.

Then again sometimes even if you did pay attention to what was happening around you it didn't do any good. The trial Cindy had recently been a juror for was a good example. The woman had noticed when her neighbors fought, had worried for the wife, but ultimately the wife had been murdered and there was nothing she could do to stop it. She was even having trouble helping put the husband in jail for it. He couldn't help but wonder when and where the trial would next take place.

Hopefully the next time they'd make it all the way through the trial without incident and convict the husband. Cindy had been sure the man was guilty and Jeremiah trusted her instincts in the matter.

It was nearing the end of the work day and traffic was getting heavier. He sped past cars, weaving in and out of lanes even as his mind raced ahead. He had spent enough time walking around the hospital in the last couple of years that he knew it pretty well. He could approach the room from an unexpected direction and have a better chance of catching whoever had the phone unaware. Hopefully nothing would have happened to Liam and Rebecca before he could get there.

~

Mark's vision was getting blurry as he struggled to fill out some paperwork at his desk. Everything was all arranged for Ruth to come and get her brother and take him to her apartment. Nothing left to worry about there. At least, not for the evening.

He tossed his pen on his desk and rubbed his temples. He could feel a headache coming on. He glanced at the clock. It was getting close to five. He should call it a day. He was no good to anyone here in the shape he was in.

He just wanted to go home, kiss Traci and the kids, and fall into bed. Even the thought of trying to choke down some dinner sounded too exhausting.

Of course, what he should do is head straight for the hospital to check on Liam and Rebecca. That was the right thing to do. What a good partner would do.

Partner.

His guts clenched at the word. Traci was right. He was worried about losing another one.

It had been nine weeks since he'd gone to Sacramento and retrieved the file on Paul from the dead attorney's private safe. In all that time he'd only looked at the papers twice. They were written in some sort of code but he hadn't had the time to try and crack it.

That's not true, a little voice seemed to whisper deep inside. He grit his teeth. Maybe he didn't want to know and that's why he hadn't managed to look at the papers more than twice in that time.

Was he really finding closure, content with what he did know about his old partner and the nightmare that must have been his childhood? No, no he wasn't.

So what was wrong with him then? If he was overwhelmed by the challenge of trying to crack the code he could have asked Jeremiah to help. The rabbi was likely far more experienced with such things. Or, he at least might know someone who was.

When it came right down to it Mark had to admit that he was afraid. Of what, he wasn't quite sure. Maybe he was afraid that when the mystery was one hundred percent solved that Paul would well and truly be gone for good. Or maybe he was afraid of finding out even worse things about his former partner.

Some things once known can't be unknown.

Just like some things couldn't be unseen.

The image of Casey sitting on the floor, rocking and holding that bloody bat was going to stick with him a long time. The image would stick with Taylor all his life.

Mark's heart went out to the officer. It wasn't an easy thing to live with, making a mistake. Taylor was lucky, though. He hadn't actually made the mistake. He hadn't fired his gun at the kid. He had gone up to the precipice and pulled back just in time.

The thing was, though, he'd had a good long look into the dark and he might not ever be the same. He might not be capable of being a cop anymore. Mark hoped that wasn't true. Taylor was a good man and they needed more like him on the force.

He'd check up on Taylor tomorrow, make sure that he was going to take the time off that Mark had suggested. He'd check up on Liam and Rebecca in a couple of hours.

First he needed to go home and kiss Traci and the kids.

And pull out a file that he'd kept locked away in a drawer in his desk. Not so that someone else couldn't steal it, but so that he couldn't accidentally come upon it.

He stood with a weary sigh. Traci was right. He needed

to be done with Paul.

~

Cindy quickly rifled through the remaining drawers in the desk after Beau left. She wanted to find all of Rose's things so she could hand the box off to Mr. Cartwright and be done with that part of things.

That would just leave the formidable task of figuring out how to file all the stacks and stacks of loose papers that decorated the desk and filled the drawers. Rose might have been great at throwing parties, but she clearly knew nothing about filing papers.

Cindy caught herself. She was thinking of Rose in the past tense. She had no proof that anything bad had happened to her despite her own misgivings and Beau's parting words to her.

She pulled a roll of packing tape out of the center drawer and taped up the box. Then she picked it up and carried it to Mr. Cartwright's office with the intention of leaving it in there for him. When she got there, though, the door was locked. Irritated, she turned around and made it back to her cubicle where she shoved it under her desk.

Next to her Leo was turning off his computer monitor.

"Time to call it a day," he said with forced cheerfulness.

She glanced at the clock on the wall. It was five 'til five. She sat down at her computer and logged off before she, too, turned off her monitor.

"See you in the morning," Leo said as he headed for the elevator.

"See you," Cindy said.

She grabbed her purse and stood up slowly, wanting to

make sure she'd given her full eight hours, silly as that seemed. All she'd accomplished for the day was cleaning out Rose's stuff and sending out a memo about people cheating the broken time clock. She probably should have asked Mr. Cartwright if she needed a timecard. It seemed like everyone else had one. She grimaced as she imagined him staring at it, trying to find a single minute that she had somehow clocked in late or clocked out early.

She shook her head. Stuff like that couldn't be good for company morale. She couldn't imagine the memo he had her send out was going to be too popular. At least it wasn't her name on it.

At exactly five o'clock she hit the call button for the elevator. Once she made it downstairs she headed for her car as swiftly as possible.

Driving out of the parking lot her mind shifted gears from the weirdness at her new job to the fact that Liam had been attacked. She hoped that they'd already caught the guy who did it and that Liam would be okay. Concern for Liam, though, wasn't what caused her to hit the accelerator a little harder than she should as she turned onto the next street. Rather it was the thought of being able to see Jeremiah shortly.

~

Jeremiah glided down the hospital hallway like a ghost, moving swiftly but taking in everything around him. He had easily passed through areas restricted to hospital staff. Security around the place really was a joke. He should have Mark suggest some upgrades.

Of course, the only time security ever seemed to be an

issue was when someone he knew was involved. At that point there wasn't a security system in the world that would actually satisfy him. If he could beat it, so could others. If he couldn't beat it, he'd worry about needing to.

Become a rabbi. That's what you planned to do before. You'll love it. It will be relaxing, like a constant vacation.

In his mind he played back phrases that he'd been told when he was being retired. His handlers clearly had not anticipated the life he'd actually end up with. Then again, how could they? Not a lot of guys lived long enough to retire from his line of work and those that did usually didn't have a need for a whole new career.

A nurse came out of Liam's room. She was walking calmly. That was a good sign. It was likely safe to enter. He hadn't seen anyone suspicious yet inside the hospital. Presumably whoever had called him was waiting in Liam's room. If they were their presence wasn't enough to upset the nursing staff.

He moved forward swiftly, ears straining to pick up any sounds from inside the room. He didn't hear any voices. He paused just shy of the doorway and gathered himself, focusing. He could feel the pressure of his gun against the small of his back. A knife was strapped to his right calf. He could reach either of them in a second.

Jeremiah stepped into the room. Liam was in the bed, eyes closed. Jeremiah glanced around, wondering where Rebecca was. He was a bit surprised that no one was there waiting for his arrival.

He stepped closer to Liam's bed. He could see his chest rising and falling gently. The younger man's eyelids flickered and a moment later he was looking up at Jeremiah. His lips began to move and Jeremiah stepped closer to better hear him.

The detective's voice was barely a whisper. "You have to help her."

"Rebecca?" Jeremiah asked.

Liam gave the barest of nods.

"What's wrong?"

"Someone is stalking her."

12

The hair on the back of Jeremiah's neck stood on end. "Someone used her phone to call me," he said.

"I did," Liam said. "She left it on the food tray."

He opened his hand to reveal the phone.

"You could have identified yourself so I didn't panic," Jeremiah said, struggling with relief and a touch of anger.

"Sorry, talking is hard. Needed you here before she got back."

"Where has she gone?"

"Food."

"Downstairs in the cafeteria?" Jeremiah guessed.

"Yes," Liam said. His voice was weaker than it had been just seconds before. His eyes closed.

"Liam, what do you want me to do?" Jeremiah asked.

Liam's eyes opened a slit. It was clear he was falling asleep and trying to fight it. "Told nurse not to..."

He drifted off as his eyes closed again.

Jeremiah stood there, hands clenched into fists at his side, as he tried to decide what to do next. A noise at the door caused him to twist around, ready to strike.

He forced himself to relax as a nurse bustled in. He moved out of her way as she grabbed Liam's chart from the foot of the bed. She glanced at it then up at Liam.

"Poor dear's finally asleep. That's good," she clucked.

"He said he told you not to do something," Jeremiah

said, raising an eyebrow.

"He asked to delay the next dose of pain medication. I told him he needed rest and he needed to stay ahead of the pain. Well, now hopefully he'll sleep through the rest of the day."

Jeremiah's frustration levels were mounting but he forced himself to smile at the woman. She was trying to be helpful even if she was getting in the way. She checked a few readings, wrote them down, then left the room.

Once she did Jeremiah moved over to Liam, took the phone from his hand, and put it back on the table next to the food tray. Then he sat down in a chair to wait. If Liam believed that Rebecca was being stalked and that it was important enough to call him and get him down there right away then he needed to talk to her as soon as she returned from lunch.

Fortunately he didn't have to wait long. She arrived within five minutes. When she stepped into the room she jerked when she saw him and half turned as though about to run.

"It's okay, it's just me, the rabbi," he said.

She stood for a moment, every line in her body taut. Then she relaxed slightly and stepped all the way into the room.

"I didn't expect to see you back here so soon," she admitted.

He raised an eyebrow. "By the looks of things you were expecting to see someone, and not a welcome visitor at that."

"No, you just startled me," she said. She glanced over anxiously at Liam.

"He just fell asleep," Jeremiah said. "The nurse finished

checking on him about five minutes ago."

"Good, he needs the rest," she said as she sat down on the edge of the chair on the opposite side of Liam from him.

The chair in which she was sitting had its back to the door and he watched as she fidgeted and glanced at least a couple of times over her shoulder in just a few seconds.

The chair he was sitting in afforded him a full view of the room, the door, and the windows even though the blinds were drawn. They hadn't been earlier. He assumed that Rebecca had done that at some point.

"Something wrong with your chair?" he asked.

"No, it's...fine," she said, trying to smile and failing.

"You look uncomfortable."

"There's nothing wrong with the chair."

"Then maybe it's the location," Jeremiah suggested calmly.

"What do you mean?" she asked, voice tightening.

"Are you cold? Is there an air conditioning vent above you?" he asked, knowing full well that there wasn't.

"No, there's...well, maybe I am a little cold," she said, changing her answer in midstream.

"We can move your chair over here."

"That would be...good," she said, hesitating as though it were hard to admit that's what she wanted.

"Here, I'll move it," he said, getting to his feet.

She hastily stood up as he walked over to grab the chair.

"I can move it," she protested.

"I've got it," he told her with a smile.

He picked up the chair and moved it around to the other side of the bed. He then angled it so it was facing Liam and him and still did not give her a good view of the door.

"There you go," he said with a smile.

"Thank you," she murmured as she sat down, turning her head to look at the door as she did so.

"You really didn't get a chance to tell me how things went with the police at your shop," Jeremiah said.

"There was just some things moved around."

"Which things? Knowing which things were moved might help the police figure out who was in there."

She twisted her head to glance toward the door and then turned back.

"I seriously doubt it. They moved all the teapots around. They pulled several packages of Earl Grey tea off the shelves. The worst damage was to a couple of tea cozies that were ripped up with something sharp."

"Anything special about those particular ones?"

She shook her head vigorously. Too much so. Jeremiah was convinced there was something special about them that she didn't want to share.

"So, not a lot of actual damage but it will require a bit of cleanup," he said.

"Pretty much."

"Any idea why your vandal would have turned around your closed sign so that it showed the store was open?"

"I don't know," she said, balling her hands into fists on the armrests of her chair.

"Did they take anything from your purse?"

"No."

"That's odd."

"There's not much in there to take," she said.

"Still, it makes it seem like it couldn't have been a thief. Otherwise they would have taken the purse or at least whatever money and credit cards you had in it."

"I guess. I don't know. Maybe whoever it was didn't find it before they left," she said.

Which was so unlikely as to be laughable. The first place anyone would look for something valuable would be behind the counter. Plus, he'd seen her purse and it had clearly been searched just like the rest of her shop.

"Did they think that it was the same person who attacked Liam?" he asked.

She went completely still. "They didn't say anything about it," she said quietly.

"Really? Given the closeness in time and proximity between the two incidents I would have thought for sure they'd be looking into connections."

Rebecca didn't say anything, but turned and glanced again at the door.

"Are you expecting someone?" Jeremiah asked.

"What? No. Why do you ask?"

"You keep looking at the door."

She flushed slightly. "Oh. I guess I'm just eager for the doctor or a nurse to come in so I can ask some more questions."

"If that's the case, I can get a nurse right now," he said, starting to rise from his chair.

"No, that's not necessary. I'm sure they'll be in when they can," she said.

Jeremiah leaned forward in his chair and pinned her with his eyes. "Rebecca?"

"Yes?" she asked, a slight quaver in her voice.

"Stop lying to me."

Rebecca blinked at Jeremiah, clearly panicking in the wake of his question. "Wh-what do you mean?" she asked.

"I know you're lying about whatever happened in your

shop this morning. Normally I'd say it was your business, but Liam here is a friend. I'm worried about him and he's worried about you. So much so, that he called me to come down here while you were in the cafeteria."

"He did?" she asked.

"Yes."

"Oh."

"I was in your store this morning. The whole place was searched, including your purse. Now, you want to tell me what's really going on?"

She turned pale. "No, I'll handle it," she said in a quiet voice.

"If this is you handling it," he said, nodding toward Liam, "you'll excuse me if I don't think that's good enough."

"Honestly, it's not your problem," she said, cheeks turning pink.

"When you started dating my best friend's partner it became my problem," he said.

"I know that you're a rabbi, but I need a lot more than a spiritual adviser," she said.

She was scared of something or someone. The more she talked the more he could see how she was thinking, feeling. He knew she'd been in the army and done two tours in Afghanistan. Theoretically not much should scare her after that. Some did come back broken, hollowed out, but she didn't strike him as that type.

He cleared his throat. "You're new in our lives. I've done my fair share to help Mark and Liam put away some criminals."

"This isn't about solving a mystery," she said.

"Then you know who's behind all this," he said.

118

Her eyes widened and her nostrils flared slightly. She'd trapped herself, honestly, but she was staring at him like a deer in the headlights. For just a moment he thought she was going to bolt and he coiled his muscles, ready to stop her if she tried.

"Do you care for Liam?" he asked.

"Yes," she said, startled.

"Then talk to him, talk to Mark, tell them what's really going on."

"The police can't help," she said softly.

"Then let me help you."

"I told you, I need more than a rabbi."

He thought of the way Liam and she had looked at each other. If they both made it through this okay then he wouldn't be surprised if there were wedding bells in their future. If that happened she'd get pulled more into the inner circle than he would like, but he couldn't begrudge Liam telling her what he knew.

He leaned forward and let his face harden. He stopped pretending for just a moment that he was only a rabbi. "And I'm telling you, I wasn't always a rabbi," he growled.

He knew she could see the change and from the way she recoiled he knew she understood on some level what it was she was seeing. Most people who saw the him that he kept hidden had the impulse to get as far away as they could.

Cindy was the exception. She had stared him down and stepped closer to him.

"I met a couple of men like you when I was overseas," Rebecca whispered.

"I very much doubt it. My kind don't mix well," he said, his voice still low.

He leaned back and let the mask fall back into place. He

smiled and she actually shivered.

"Does Liam know?" she asked.

"He knows enough to ask me to come down here and help fix things," Jeremiah said, still smiling as if there was nothing wrong in the entire world.

She turned and looked at Liam. "Everything is so messed up," she whimpered.

Jeremiah heard a familiar step in the hall just outside Liam's room.

"Cindy's here," he said.

Rebecca turned toward the door. Moments later Cindy appeared and stepped inside.

Jeremiah felt his heart start to beat faster just at the sight of her. He stood to his feet as though compelled and crossed the room to take her in his arms and hug her tight.

"Are you okay?" she whispered.

"I am now," he said.

Every time he had to think about his past he needed her to pull him back out of it. He breathed her scent in deeply. She'd used strawberry shampoo on her hair. He loved it when she did that. He should probably tell her so.

Reluctantly he let her go and stepped back. She gave him a shaky smile. Her day hadn't gone well, he could tell. That made two of them.

She turned and looked at Liam. "Is he going to be okay?"

"We'll know for sure in forty-eight hours," Jeremiah told her. "There was some damage to his liver and spleen so now it's just a waiting game."

"He's not in a coma, is he?" she asked.

He knew she was thinking about when she'd almost lost her brother a while back. "No, Liam was awake a little bit ago, but they gave him pain medication so he could rest which is what he needs more than anything," he hastened to tell her.

"Okay," she said, visibly relaxing a bit.

"And this is Liam's girlfriend, Rebecca," Jeremiah said, turning to introduce them. "Rebecca, this is my fiancée, Cindy."

"It's nice to meet you. Traci has said some wonderful things about you," Cindy said as she shook her hand.

"And Liam talks about you all the time," Rebecca said, forcing a smile.

Jeremiah couldn't help but compare the two women. Cindy overcame her fears all the time, thriving in adversity. Rebecca was on the verge of succumbing to hers. Given their two backgrounds it would have been logical to assume the opposite. Cindy, though, was special. She had learned to triumph even when the odds were all against her.

"So, where are we on finding out who did this?" Cindy asked.

That's my girl, he thought proudly.

"Actually, Rebecca and I were just about to get into that," he said.

"Please, ladies, sit," Jeremiah said, steering Cindy toward the chair he'd vacated. "As it turns out, someone searched Rebecca's shop while she was headed to the hospital with Liam."

"That's terrible! Same guy? That's too big a coincidence otherwise," Cindy said.

"That's what I thought. Rebecca, care to tell us anything?" he asked pointedly.

"No," she said.

"Okay," he said. He turned to Cindy. "Liam thinks

someone is stalking her."

"That's terrible! Have you told the police?" Cindy asked.

"I'm guessing she hasn't. Liam actually asked me not to tell the police," Jeremiah said.

"Even Mark? That makes no sense."

Jeremiah shrugged. "Not at the moment."

He turned back to Rebecca and narrowed his eyes. "Well?"

She dropped her eyes. "I don't know. I think it's possible, that someone might be stalking me. I pray I'm wrong. I *have* to be wrong," she said, her voice cracking.

"Why is that?" Cindy asked.

Rebecca looked up with haunted eyes. She gestured slowly to Liam. "Because if I'm right, this is just the beginning."

13

Cindy's heart went out to Rebecca. The other woman was clearly terrified. "You have to tell us what you know so that we can stop him," she urged.

"There's no stopping him," Rebecca said as a tear rolled down her cheek.

"Yes, there is. There's not a man alive who can stand up to Jeremiah," Cindy said fervently.

She saw Jeremiah wince at that.

"You don't understand. He's former army, special forces."

"Tell me about him," Jeremiah said, his voice low and dangerous sounding.

Chills danced up Cindy's spine. She'd seen firsthand what Jeremiah could do and she didn't give the stalker even three seconds to survive a fight with him.

Rebecca just turned pale and shook her head. She clearly didn't want to talk although why Cindy didn't know. Was she protecting him? That seemed unlikely given how afraid of him she was and given what he'd done to Liam.

She was about to press the matter when Jeremiah abruptly stood. Rebecca looked as startled as she felt.

"Cindy, I think it's time you and I got something to eat. We can finish discussing this afterward," he said.

She wanted to protest but she was hungry and certain

that he must have a good reason for delaying the rest of the conversation.

"I could eat," she said, standing up.

Jeremiah scooped a phone up off Liam's bedside table and tossed it to Rebecca who caught it. "We're going to be downstairs in the cafeteria. Call if anything happens," he said.

Rebecca nodded mutely and Jeremiah grabbed Cindy's arm and steered her out of the room. They headed down the hallway outside and got on an elevator. Once the doors had closed she turned to him.

"What was that?"

"We weren't going to get anything more out of her at the moment. She's more scared to talk than she is to stay quiet at this point. I'm hoping that some time alone with Liam in that hospital room will flip that."

"Why do you think she's too scared to talk?" Cindy asked.

"I don't know, but figuring that out might help."

The doors opened and they stepped out into another corridor and headed for the cafeteria.

"Liam called me to come down here and told me not to bring any cops."

"That's weird, why?"

"I don't know. The nurse had just given him something to sleep when I got here. All he had time to tell me was that he thought Rebecca was being stalked."

"It's weird. Why call you instead of Mark?"

"I don't know," Jeremiah admitted as they reached the cafeteria.

"Well, it's a lot crazier than my imagined work mystery," Cindy said.

Jeremiah turned to gaze quizzically at her. "What imagined work mystery?"

"I'll tell you once we sit down," she said.

~

Ten minutes later Jeremiah and Cindy were sitting down with their food selections at a table in the back corner. The food was bland but at least it was fuel.

"So, what happened at work today?" he asked as Cindy picked up a piece of fried chicken.

"I'm pretty sure I invented an entire mystery surrounding the woman who worked at my desk before I did."

"Oh? How so?" he asked, taking a bite of his meatloaf.

"I was asked to pack up all her personal items that she left behind. There was a lot of it, too. Pictures, articles of clothing, a necklace. You name it, and she left it."

"That's a bit odd."

"More than a bit," Cindy said. "Apparently Friday after work she was all smiles, but then she never showed up for work yesterday."

"Ah, strange, but weirder things have happened."

"True, but I ran into a coworker who was just as shocked as I was and very determined to find out what had happened to her. He was sure she hadn't quit and insisted that something had happened to her."

"Did this coworker have her contact information?"

"Unfortunately not. He was hoping I did."

"Okay, and did you?"

"No! I still don't. Can you believe my boss insisted on mailing it personally rather than giving me the address?"

125

"That is weird."

"Yeah, and on top of being a jerk he's lazy. So it doesn't make sense that he wanted to take care of that or anything else."

Jeremiah took a swig of soda. "So, not liking your new boss much?"

"You can say that again. The whole place just gives me the creeps," she admitted.

"Fortunately you don't have to stay very long."

"So, what do you think?"

"About the disappearing secretary? I don't know," Jeremiah admitted.

"Me either. Well, maybe tomorrow will make everything clearer."

"I hope so."

"How do you want to handle Rebecca?" Cindy asked, changing subjects.

Jeremiah sighed. "That is an excellent question."

~

Mark walked in his front door. Buster was right there to greet him with a tail wag and a happy bark. He gave the dog a few pets before heading into the kitchen. Traci, unfortunately, looked less happy to see him than Buster had. He couldn't blame her since it had been an upsetting day all around. Even still, she was a sight for sore eyes.

He walked straight up to her, wrapped his arms around her, and buried his face against her neck. He shuddered slightly as he tried to push out of his mind the horrors of the day. A moment later he felt Traci's arms come up around him, holding him. She slowly rubbed his back and began to make soothing noises.

"It's okay," she whispered.

He held her tighter, never wanting to let go. He didn't know how long they stood there like that but when he finally released her and stepped back he could see that there were tears in her eyes.

"I'm so sorry," he said, a wave of guilt washing over him.

"For what?" she asked.

"For everything. For my crazy job and the stress and horror I bring home with me. For the risks I take. For just, I don't know-"

She leaned forward and kissed him. When it was over she smiled sadly up at him. "You're not the one who got hurt," she said.

"Yeah, but I have been in the past. And I've hurt others," he said.

She put her hand on his cheek and caressed it. "Mark, you're tired."

He nodded. He was and it was making him think crazy things. He thought about Liam laying in that hospital bed. He replayed the images of Casey sitting on the ground holding the bloody bat that had killed his parents and Taylor breaking down and trying to surrender his badge and gun to Mark after nearly shooting Casey. It just felt suddenly like all too much.

"What if I quit?" he blurted out.

Traci's eyes opened wide. "Excuse me?"

"What if I quit my job, stopped being a cop?"

She blinked rapidly, as though trying to process what he was saying. "And do what?"

"I don't know. I could become a lawyer."

"You hated school," she pointed out.

That was true. Plus as a lawyer he'd still have to deal with all the crap that he wanted away from so badly at that moment. "Okay, I could go into private security. I could be Joseph's bodyguard or something."

A short, explosive laugh erupted from Traci.

"What's so funny about that?" he asked.

"You think that would be safer? Have you met our friends?"

He hung his head and let out a frustrated sigh. She was right about that. Their friends, Joseph included, managed to have an amazing amount of bad things happen to and around them.

Traci put her hand under his chin and forced his head up. She looked him in the eyes. "Look, honey, if you want to quit and do something else, then okay, we can figure that out."

"I sense a 'but' coming," he said.

She nodded. "But, are you sure this isn't just about Paul and Liam's condition dredging all that up again?"

"It was a pretty bad day," he said, barely getting the words out.

"I understand. And we can talk about it. And ultimately if you want to quit and do something else I'm for it, one hundred percent. I just don't want you making a hasty decision you're going to regret later," she said.

It was pretty much the same advice he'd given Taylor. It had been good advice for the other man and it was good advice for him as well.

"Thank you."

Traci smiled at him sweetly. "That's what I'm here for," she said.

In the other room the babies began to cry. "And you're here to take care of them while I finish up dinner," she said with a smirk.

"Thanks," he said sarcastically.

~

After dinner Traci settled down with the twins in the living room. They were playing on the floor while she watched a movie. As much as Mark wanted to join them he knew he needed to deal with a few things. So instead he headed into his office.

Reluctantly he unlocked the one drawer and pulled out his file on Paul, or, rather, Not Paul as he sometimes referred to him. In it he found the twelve pages written in code that he'd gotten from the attorney's safe plus the one that had been in the letter the attorney had sent to Georgia, Paul's ex-wife. Mark spread them out on his desk and stared at them.

What secrets could they be holding? Was it just what he'd already managed to piece together on his own or was there more?

In the folder there was also an envelope with a key that Paul's lawyer had sent to Paul's ex-wife when he died. He still had no idea what that key went to.

"I can do this. I'm a detective after all," he said out loud, trying to psyche himself up.

He grabbed a pencil and blank piece of paper and tried to work out what the code might be. He started with the most frequent letter that he found and called it an "e" since "e" was the most frequently used letter in English. He worked through as far with that as he could, but it became clear very quickly that this was not a simple substitution cipher like they had in puzzle books.

As he stared at the papers his frustration grew. He could read a crime scene with surprising ease and accuracy at this point. Codes, though, were not his thing. Leave it to Paul to make it difficult. It seemed there was nothing in the man's life that hadn't been.

Mark sat there for a couple of more minutes and then got onto his computer and found a website about secret codes since the simple substitution was all that he was familiar with. His mind began to boggle as he scrolled through the information. Finally he turned away from his computer. The only clear thing that had emerged was that he needed help.

He put the pages through his printer/copier and then put the originals back in his drawer, locking it again. Then he called Jeremiah.

"Hello?" the rabbi answered, sounding tired.

It had been a long day for everyone.

"How are you at breaking codes?" Mark asked without preamble.

"What kind of codes?"

"That's the problem, I'm not sure."

"Breaking them has never exactly been my area of expertise," the other man admitted.

"Oh," Mark said, feeling discouragement settle upon him.

"Hold on a second," Jeremiah said suddenly.

Mark waited. He could hear muffled voices but couldn't make out what anyone was saying. Finally Jeremiah came back on.

"We've got a couple of people here who'd like to take a

crack at what you've got," he said.

"Oh? And where are you at?"

"The hospital. Where are you at?"

Mark flushed. Jeremiah was still watching over his partner, the one he hadn't had the strength or will to go see before coming straight home. "On my way there," he mumbled into the phone before hanging up.

He grabbed the copies of the papers, told Traci where he was going, and headed for the hospital. He was half asleep as he drove, the car seeming to almost drive itself. It felt like he spent an inordinate amount of time there anymore.

"Oh look, the gang's all here," he said when he walked into Liam's room to find Rebecca, Jeremiah, and Cindy there.

"Hey, Mark," Cindy said.

He nodded in greeting.

There was one chair left and he sat down in it before turning to look at Liam. His partner's eyes were closed.

"Nurse gave him something to knock him out a few hours ago," Jeremiah said. "He's been fighting it, drifting in and out the last hour."

"Why fight it? Sleep has to be the best thing for him at this point," Mark said. "Besides, there's nothing he can do to help."

"That's not entirely true," Jeremiah spoke up.

"He remembered something about the guy who attacked him?" Mark asked hopefully.

"No, but he did make a pertinent observation," Cindy said uncomfortably.

Mark looked around at all of them. There was something they weren't telling him.

"Come on, guys, what was it? Fill me in."

Liam's eyes flew open. "No cops!" he snarled in a voice that was barely recognizable.

14

Mark nearly jumped out of his skin when Liam spoke. Jeremiah had to admit to being suddenly on edge himself.

"What are you talking about?" Mark said. "I'm a cop. *You're* a cop."

"Don't tell him. He's a cop," Liam said.

"What the hell has gotten into you?" Mark exploded.

Liam just closed his eyes and said nothing.

Mark rounded on Rebecca. "Tell me what's going on *right now*!"

Jeremiah stood up. "Mark, I'm not sure what's going on, but I think we'll deal with it. Maybe it's best if we all got some rest tonight. I think we're all on edge."

Mark glared at him but he could tell that his words were making sense to the detective.

"Fine," he finally snapped. He turned to go, a sheath of papers still tucked under his arm.

"Mark, you had something you wanted decoded?" Jeremiah gently reminded him.

Mark turned back. "I thought you said that wasn't your area?"

"It isn't, but Liam and Rebecca apparently have both had some experience with it."

Mark's face hardened even more.

"I'd like to try and help. It will give me...us...something to do while we're stuck here," Rebecca said.

Mark turned and for a moment Jeremiah was afraid he was going to do or say something incredibly rash. Instead he took a deep breath. He handed her the papers.

"No one but the four of you sees these," he said.

"Understood."

"I will be back in the morning to discuss all of this," he said, indicating her and Liam with a sweeping arm gesture.

She nodded but didn't say anything.

Mark glanced at Jeremiah. "I'm going home to get some rest. I suggest you do the same."

"Good night," Cindy said.

Mark grunted and left the room.

"I think we should go as well," Jeremiah said. He wasn't getting anything more out of either of them that night. At this point everyone was too keyed up. Emotions were running high and no one was thinking straight. Better to start again when more rational thought might prevail.

He and Cindy left the hospital room.

"Is this goodnight?" she asked hesitantly.

"Nah, I'll come over to your house and we can talk some more," he said.

"Good."

~

"Well, that was...something," Cindy said as they walked into her house.

Jeremiah closed and locked the door behind him then followed her into the living room.

Cindy sat down on the couch wearily and looked up at Jeremiah. He looked tired, too. It was something he rarely showed. After a few seconds he sat down on the couch beside her.

They sat in companionable silence for a couple of minutes. She glanced at the clock on the wall. It was eight. She should send him on his way. The morning was going to come soon and she was tired enough to sleep right through it.

She glanced around the room.

"You know, I've never really felt like this was my house," she said.

"Oh, why?"

"I'm not sure. I mean, it's been a while since I inherited it, but it just still doesn't feel like I own it."

"Paint one of the walls and see if that changes," he said with a wry smile.

She chuckled. "But how will I get my security deposit back?"

He laughed, too. After a few seconds it died down. "You know what you could do?"

"What?"

"Change one of the pictures on the walls."

She looked around and flushed slightly. He was right. The art prints were the ones she'd inherited along with the house. They were nice, neutral landscapes and for some reason she'd left them up.

The bedroom that Geanie had stayed in when they were roommates was a blank canvas because they had either moved or gotten rid of the few things that had been there. The rest of the house, though, was virtually untouched. Even the couch they were sitting on had come with the house.

A wave of sorrow suddenly washed over her and a tear rolled down her cheek.

"What's wrong?" Jeremiah asked.

"It's silly really. I spent the day packing up Rose's things. It just struck me that it's probably time to pack up Marge's things."

"The lady who left you the house?" Jeremiah asked.

"Yeah," Cindy said, dashing away the tear. "I wonder if she would have done that if she'd known I was going to stop being the church secretary?"

Jeremiah put a hand on her shoulder. "She left you this house not because you were the church secretary but because she cared for you. From what I understand you were the one who visited her most faithfully the last year she was alive."

"She was a nice lady. She had some great stories and no one to share them with," Cindy said.

"She got to share them with you and I'm sure that meant the world to her," he said gently.

Cindy nodded. It really had been a long day.

"You know what, don't worry about it. We can tackle it together after I move in," he said.

"Move in?" she asked, startled.

He raised an eyebrow. "In twenty months? After the wedding I kind of figured we'd live in the same place. It's customary here in America, I understand."

She just kept staring at him, at a loss for words.

He shifted uncomfortably. "My house is much smaller and owned by a synagogue member, not me. Therefore, I assumed I'd be moving in here. I'm sorry, did I overstep?" he asked, looking suddenly worried.

"No, it's just...this is going to sound weird...I hadn't really thought much past the wedding," she said.

"That's okay," he said with a sly grin. "I haven't

thought much past the honeymoon."

She grabbed a pillow off the couch and hit him with it. She tried to hit him a second time but he easily caught it and then pulled her into his arms.

He kissed her and everything else seemed to fall away. When the kiss ended she put her head on his chest and enjoyed the feeling of him just holding her.

"Of course you'll be moving in here after the wedding," she said. "You can have the guest room."

"Don't make me tickle you," he threatened.

She giggled, feeling a happy warmth stealing over her.

"I guess there's a lot of things that you and I haven't had a chance to discuss that most couples have by this point," he said after a minute.

"You're probably right," she said.

He kissed the top of her head.

"How many children do you want?" she asked.

His arms tightened around her. "I don't know," he said, sounding a little breathless. "How many do you want?"

"One or two. It would be nice to have a boy and a girl. Although having just one could be nice, too." She twisted her head so she could look up into his face. "Why don't you know how many you want?"

He looked down at her. "To be honest, I never thought I was going to be able to have children."

"Able? Why, is there something...wrong?" she asked.

"Sorry, no, not that I'm aware of. I just never thought I would be married and so I never thought children were in my future."

"Well, you *are* going to be married, so start thinking about it," she said.

"Yes, ma'am."

"Since you mentioned the honeymoon, where do you think we should go?" she asked.

"Somewhere that we can be totally alone," he said.

"Really? And why is that?" she asked, unable to keep the amusement out of her voice.

"Because I have serious, serious plans for us."

"Oh really, like what?" she teased.

"I plan on taking off my clothes," he said.

"Yeah?" she asked, unable to stop the grin that was spreading across her face.

"Yes," he said, but his face was growing more serious, the lighthearted tone he'd been speaking in was changing.

"And?" she asked.

"And I'm going to tell you exactly how I got each one of my scars."

She sat up. That had not been what she was expecting. "You are?" she asked in surprise.

He nodded solemnly. "You've earned hearing those stories."

"Thank you, I'm honored, and I look forward to hearing the stories."

"But, what?" he asked.

She blushed. "I just had something else in mind when you said you were going to take your clothes off."

"Yeah, like what?" he asked with a straight face.

Staring at him she felt tongue-tied and far too shy to voice the thoughts in her mind. Suddenly she saw a wicked little gleam in Jeremiah's eyes. He pulled her close again and nuzzled her throat.

He began to whisper against her skin. "Maybe you thought that I was going to say that then I'd unzip your dress and let it fall to the floor. I'd run my hands across your bare skin until you began to tremble. Then I'd pick you up and carry you to the bed. Is that what you were thinking about?" he asked.

"Yes," she managed to say.

She twisted her hands in his hair and he kissed her throat and jaw before kissing her lips again. Sudden heat flashed through her. His lips kept roaming, moving on to her cheeks.

"Why can't we do that now?" she asked breathlessly.

"Because we're not married," he said as he kept kissing her, trailing kisses down to the other side of her neck.

"We should get married."

"I couldn't agree more," he said as he nuzzled her ear.

"I'm serious," she groaned.

"So am I."

"I'm tired of waiting."

"So am I," he said before kissing her lips again.

"Let's get married tonight," she said.

He pulled away just enough so he could look her in the eyes. "You can't be serious," he said.

"I am," she said.

He brushed the hair out of her face. "I need you to think right now."

She shook her head. "I think too much."

"Usually, yes, but not now. Why do you want to elope tonight?"

"You know why," she said, leaning forward to kiss him.

"Cindy, if that's what you really want, we'll go tonight," he said, pulling back. "We'll drive to Nevada and we'll get married. But I need you to be honest with me. Is this just about wanting to have sex?"

"I want to get married," she said.

"So do I, but I'm talking about right now. Do you want to get married tonight instead of next December because you want us to have sex?"

"Yes," she said.

He closed his eyes and looked like he was struggling with himself. Then he opened his eyes again. "And afterward, will you be sorry we didn't have a real wedding with our friends there?"

"I...I don't know," she admitted.

"I think you will be. And I'm not going to rob you of the wedding just so we both get what we want tonight. It's not worth it."

"I want you," she told him, throat constricting.

"And I promise you that if I thought we wouldn't regret it, you'd have me before the night was over."

She whimpered low in her throat. He stroked her face. "I know it's hard. I also know that in twenty months when we rip each other's clothes off it will have been worth the wait."

She licked her lips. She knew what he was saying made sense, even though she didn't want to admit it.

"Back in Israel, after...everything...you told me that you belonged to me, that I could have whatever I wanted. I knew what you meant. You would have that night."

"Yes, I would have," he said. "And that night you were strong for both of us. Tonight I'll be the one who is strong for both of us."

"I don't want you to be," she admitted.

"Which is exactly why I have to be," he said. He moved and then stood up. "And the only way I can do that right now is to go."

"Please, don't go," she said, tears filling her eyes.

She didn't know what was wrong with her, why she was feeling so vulnerable. She thought about him, them, all the time, but somehow tonight a feeling of desperation had crept over her.

He crouched down next to her. "Look me in the eyes and tell me that you will never regret not having a real wedding. You won't regret standing in the front of the church and reciting our vows with you in a white dress and me in a tuxedo. You won't regret everyone cheering and wishing us well. You won't regret cutting the cake at the reception and trying to feed it to each other."

"I would regret it," she finally whispered.

He kissed her forehead. "Then let's not do anything we're going to regret."

She nodded but stayed on the couch while he saw himself out.

~

Jeremiah barely made it to his car before his knees gave way. He leaned against it, shaking uncontrollably. He wished with everything in him that they were both there, heading for Nevada, about to be married. He didn't want to wait. He wouldn't regret not having the big wedding. All he wanted was to be with her always and forever. He loved her too much, though, to rob her of what she truly wanted.

Shortly after Jeremiah left, Cindy got ready for bed. She felt melancholy, but kept trying to cheer herself up with thinking about the wedding. It didn't work, though, and she finally had to admit that she was just in some kind of funky mood.

Once in bed she tossed and turned for two hours, but sleep wouldn't come. She finally got up and after getting a glass of orange juice sat down at her computer. She figured she'd surf the internet for a few minutes. Instead she headed straight for Facebook. She had an account although she never used it. She clicked on the search box at the top.

What was Rose's last name? she asked herself as her fingers hovered over the keyboard.

She had seen it on several things that day, including the insurance documents sent to her. She tried to picture the envelope in her mind. A moment later she typed *Rose Meyer* into the search box with satisfaction.

A few names popped up so she added *Rayburn NextGen Solutions* to the search. It worked. A page came up and the banner was the same picture that she'd seen earlier of Rose sitting on Santa's lap. Rose didn't have the security settings on to keep non-friends from seeing her posts which was a relief.

Cindy felt a bit guilty for her own cyber stalking, but she couldn't let it go. Not just yet. She hastily scrolled through the posts. It looked like Rose normally posted something on her page two or three times a day. However, the most recent post was Thursday night. There was nothing since then. Four days with absolutely nothing.

It doesn't necessarily mean anything, she told herself in her sternest inner voice. Rose could easily be away from her computer, staying with friends or going on a vacation now that she had the free time.

She moved the mouse and the cursor hovered for a moment over the button to send a private message. She stared at it for several seconds. She could message her, ask if she was alright, and tell her that she'd be having her things sent to her. It sounded better than just asking if she was still alive.

Of course, she might not answer just because she doesn't know who I am, she thought.

She moved the cursor and shook her head in disgust. Now that would definitely be taking cyber stalking too far. Besides, Beau had probably already done that. After all, he seemed like the kind of guy who left no stone unturned. If he confronted her again she'd ask him.

She closed down the page in disgust and forced herself to down her orange juice and head back to bed.

I'm just trying to find excuses why I should quit this job, she thought to herself. *You know, I don't need excuses. I could just do it, tell the temp agency that the boss gave me the creeps or something like that.*

She couldn't do that. The temp agency might not want to risk sending her out on another job, even if she'd already successfully accomplished a few others. She couldn't risk her future work possibilities.

As she crawled into bed another thought occurred to her. *Maybe I'm not trying to find excuses to leave but I'm trying to find reasons to stay and not go out of my mind doing so.*

Stranger things had happened. She had to admit that the possibility of a mystery surrounding Rose's abrupt departure from the company had nicely pulled her attention away from just how much she disliked Mr. Cartwright and how miserable working for him for a few weeks was going to be.

She wasn't sure which reason for her obsession made her more pathetic.

Blackie got up, stretched, came over and flopped down next to her stomach. As she scratched the cat's belly he began to purr. She always found his purr to be a very soothing sound. She forced herself to focus on it until she drifted off to sleep.

15

There was no way Jeremiah was sleeping. When he'd gotten home he'd taken a cold shower then tried to watch some television. Every single channel, though, seemed to be airing a show or movie that had gratuitous sex in it. He finally gave up and took another cold shower.

He often suspected that most women had very little idea how they impacted men, drove them crazy. Cindy in particular. There had been times where she'd intentionally tried to turn him on, and, few as they were, they were quite memorable. What she didn't realize was that most days just being in her presence was enough. Hearing her laugh, seeing her skirt swish slightly around her knees when she walked, even the way she sometimes unconsciously flipped her hair all drove him to distraction.

It was going to be a long twenty months. That was okay. He would just try and focus on other things.

Like what it was Liam and Rebecca weren't telling them. He knew he'd told Cindy and Mark that they should tackle the problem in the morning when everyone was a little more rested. That plan went right out the window, though. If he couldn't sleep then he was going to share his misery with someone else.

It only took a few minutes to drive to the hospital. It was nearly midnight and the streets were deserted. Once there he walked straight through the lobby like he belonged there and no one questioned his passing.

The hospital had been transitioning away from having traditional visiting hours to a more open policy that allowed relatives to spend the night if they wished. It helped him since no one bothered to stop him and ask what he was doing there so late at night.

There was a policeman stationed outside Liam's room. He wasn't directly outside the door, but rather sitting in a chair about five feet away reading a newspaper.

With a disgusted eye roll Jeremiah didn't even bother trying to be sneaky. He just walked right in.

Liam was asleep. Rebecca was sitting at a small desk with Mark's papers spread out before her. She had a mug of what was likely tea sitting to one side. She was concentrating so hard that she didn't even realize he was there until he cleared his throat.

She let out a yelp and jumped. "Oh, it's you," she panted in relief, placing a hand on her chest.

"A good thing, too, given how seriously the cop out there is taking his lookout duties."

She grimaced.

Jeremiah pulled up a chair. "Any luck on the code?"

"No. I did some code work in the army, but this is just gibberish to me. Hopefully Liam will have better luck when he wakes up."

"You mean *if* he wakes up," Jeremiah said darkly.

Rebecca started as though struck.

"And, of course, if he doesn't you know it's your fault."

"Why would you say that?" she whispered.

"Because, it's true. If he hadn't started dating you none of this would have happened to him, would it?" Jeremiah asked.

"I'm the victim here!"

"I'm sorry. You were the victim. Now that you're refusing to speak up and help catch the guy who did this you're looking more and more like an accessory."

"That's a lie!" she hissed.

"Okay, then tell me what the truth is," he challenged.

She looked down and he knew instinctively that he had her.

"His name is Mason. He was special forces. I met him overseas. He seemed nice, attentive. Soon we were dating."

"And?" Jeremiah asked.

"And then, after a while, his true colors came out. He was possessive, controlling, jealous. He put a guy in the hospital just for asking me what time it was. He was insane. I broke it off with him. He didn't like that, but fortunately I was heading back home. When I made it back to the states I got out of the military and got as far away from my former life as I could, just to be on the safe side. You know anything about that?" she asked.

"I do," he admitted.

"I thought I was fine. Life went on. I opened my tea shop and then I met Liam. It felt like I really had been able to start off fresh, leave the bad behind me."

"Until it found you."

She nodded.

"When did you know?"

"The last couple of days I've felt funny, you know when it's like you can feel someone watching you, but you can't tell who?"

Jeremiah nodded.

"There was nothing I could actually put my finger on. I thought I was just jumpy. Then Liam was attacked and I was just so scared I wasn't even thinking about it."

"Until?"

"Until I went back to my shop today to talk with the police."

"What did you find?"

"In my purse I had a picture of Liam and me. It had been torn in half and the half with Liam stolen. Then there was a section of teas that was undisturbed. It seemed odd to me since everything else seemed to have been jostled. When I went to take a closer look I saw that someone had left me a message, written in loose tea leaves, on the top of the boxes."

"What did it say?" he asked.

"It said, *Miss me?* That's when I thought that it had to be Mason. I don't know how he found me, but I think he searched my shop and I think he beat up Liam."

"And why didn't you want to tell the police this?" Jeremiah asked.

She cleared her throat. "One of the officers who was helping me spooked me a bit. He kept saying the oddest little things, weird, chilling comments. I started to think that maybe he knew Mason in some way. I even wondered if he's how Mason found me."

"Which officer?"

"I don't know his name, but it spooked me. I told Liam. He got really strange about it, muttering about not trusting cops. He didn't seem in his right mind, but he was so adamant...that's why I didn't want to say anything to Mark."

Jeremiah just stared at her.

"I know it sounds weird, believe me, I get that, but I'm telling you the truth."

"I believe you. I'm just not sure that Mark will."

~

It was a new morning and Mark felt better. Traci had blessedly handled the children all night so that he could just sleep. At her insistence he'd worn a pair of earplugs and hadn't heard a thing until she woke him in the morning because his alarm was going off.

He planned to swing by the hospital first to check in on Liam and, presumably, Rebecca. Then he was heading to Ruth's house to check on her and Casey.

He pulled into the hospital parking lot and parked. He got out of the car and headed toward the front doors only to stop in his tracks.

Jeremiah was standing there, arms folded across his chest. He saw Mark and dropped his arms as he walked toward him.

"To what do I owe the pleasure?" Mark asked.

Jeremiah looked like he'd been up all night. "Just thought I'd save you the trip inside," he said.

"Why?" Mark asked suspiciously.

"Because it's going to be a busy day. The name of the man who's likely stalking Rebecca is Mason Dunwoody, former special forces."

"Uh huh," Mark said, reaching into his pocket for his pen and notebook to write it down. "And why, pray tell, could she not have divulged that last night?"

"She's a bit paranoid. She thinks one of the officers who was at her shop yesterday kept acting odd, saying strange things until she wondered if he knew Mason."

"Which one?"

"She doesn't know his name and she's not much help with a description either. She was just too freaked out."

"Okay, but he wasn't the one in the hospital room last night."

"That's where things get weirder."

"Oh, great, I always love it when that happens," Mark said sarcastically.

"She told Liam and he started muttering about not trusting cops. She said he was acting oddly and that it was him who insisted they not involve the police."

"That makes no sense," Mark said.

"It doesn't make sense to her either."

"How about to you?"

Jeremiah shrugged. "I've been wondering just how bad his head injury is."

"I'm not sure I can deal with this right now," Mark admitted.

"I know, which is why I'm trying to help."

Mark sighed. "You got anything else for me?"

"Rebecca can't make sense of the coded pages. She's hoping when he's a bit more lucid that Liam can make something of them."

"Alright. Well, I'll get people looking for Mason Dunwoody. Keep me informed of any changes."

"I'm actually heading home to grab a shower and then go to work. I'll be swinging by here for lunch, though, and again after work."

"Good to know. Okay, I'll keep you informed about any changes. How's that?" Mark asked.

"Works for me."

~

Cindy was at her desk in the morning five minutes before she had to be. Even though she didn't have a time card to punch, at least not yet, the memo she'd had to send out the day before had made her a bit paranoid.

Leo staggered in looking a bit worse for wear and gave her a nod. He fell into his chair rather ingloriously.

"Are you okay?" she asked.

He yawned so hard it shook his entire body. "Bachelor party last night."

"Yours or a friend's?"

He grimaced. "Heavens, not mine. It was for ...more of an acquaintance really."

"On a Tuesday night? Isn't that a bit odd?"

"*He's* a bit odd," she heard him mutter. He shook himself. "Nah, it was something about the only day the best man could make it work. To be honest, I don't think I even remember half the night."

Cindy didn't say anything even though she wondered how drunk he must have been. She couldn't help but wonder what Jeremiah's bachelor party was going to be like. She was pretty sure that heavy drinking would *not* be a feature of the evening. Jeremiah didn't drink. With his background that was definitely for the best.

She then thought about her bachelorette party. She had been responsible for Geanie's which had gotten hijacked by the crazed killer that was trying to ruin Geanie and Joseph's wedding. The party had ended up being even tamer than Cindy had imagined. Just as well given all that was going on that week.

She couldn't help but wonder if Geanie was going to take the opportunity to go over the top for hers. Her friend had a history of loving big, theatrical things.

She sighed. There was plenty of time for worrying about that sort of thing later. After all, they had an entire twenty months before they were getting married. There were days where that didn't feel like enough time to really plan and other days where that seemed like the most interminable wait in the world.

She kept glancing toward the elevator, waiting for Mr. Cartwright to show up so she'd know what she was doing with her day. Twenty minutes later she decided to start trying to make a filing system for the papers that Rose had left in seemingly random stacks all over the desk and piled in the drawers.

The morning progressed slowly. She finally asked Leo if he knew when Mr. Cartwright would be in but he just shrugged and swallowed some aspirin. Just before noon he took off to go to lunch and she kept trying to create a workable filing system. She had found a box of file folders in one of the cabinets near the printer and she set about putting them to good use.

An hour later things were starting to finally take shape in that area. Cindy looked at the clock. She wanted to take lunch a little late, but not quite as late as she had on Tuesday. She had no idea where in the building Beau worked but she hoped to catch him in the lunchroom again. She had some questions that she was hoping he could answer.

She finally headed down there. She approached the lunchroom quickly, rehearsing what she'd say to him if he was there. She stepped into the room and noticed that the only person in there was a man who was just turning away from the microwave. She wasn't certain, but thought it might be him.

"Beau," she said softly.

He stiffened and then turned all the way. There were dark circles under his eyes like he hadn't slept much the night before. That made two of them. He had a cup of ramen noodles in his hand. He looked at her warily.

"Oh, hi, um..."

"Hi," she said, forcing a smile. "It's Cindy."

He cleared his throat. "Cindy, right. Look, I'm sorry if I scared you when I confronted you."

"It's okay," she told him. "It's fine."

"No, it's really not. I was in a bad place...not quite thinking straight," he said with a grimace.

"I've been there," she said.

He raised an eyebrow. "You've stood there screaming at a total stranger to help you find your missing friend?"

Cindy shrugged. "Close enough that you might be surprised."

"Huh. Okay," he said, setting the cup of ramen down on one of the tables and pulling out a chair.

Cindy pulled up a chair at the same table and began to take her lunch out of the brown bag she'd brought it in.

"Rose must be very special," she said, having to remind herself not to talk about the woman in the past tense.

"Very special," he said. "I've never met anyone like her. She was so giving, always looking out for other people. She'd listen to everyone. If you needed to talk, she was there. So many people are only nice if they think they'll get something out of it. Not her, she was the genuine thing."

Cindy noticed that while she wasn't referring to Rose in the past tense Beau certainly was.

"You think something happened to her, don't you?"

He hesitated then nodded slowly.

"Why?"

"I don't know, just a feeling in my gut. Like deep down I know that something's wrong, that I've lost...her," he said, choking back emotion at the end.

"Do you have any idea what might have happened?"

"No, but I want to know. I *need* to know," he said.

"You loved her, didn't you?" she asked softly.

"Yes," he whispered.

"Did you ever tell her?"

"No. I wanted to, a dozen times, but it was never right."

"Why not?" Cindy pressed.

"She had a lot she was dealing with last year," he said. "Her grandmother was sick for most of it. She was everything to Rose. She raised her."

Cindy thought of the picture of Rose and the older woman that she had carefully packed away in the box.

"What happened?"

"She died, toward the beginning of October. Rose was in a lot of pain, grieving. I tried to be her friend, to listen to her, but I couldn't be *that guy*."

"That guy?" Cindy questioned.

"Yeah, you know, the guy who takes advantage of girls when they're grieving. I didn't want to tell her how I felt because I was afraid either she would think that I was just trying to get close to her or she would react just out of her own pain and not because she cared for me, too."

"That's very honorable of you," she said.

"Yeah, been thinking a lot in the last couple of days that maybe I shouldn't have been so honorable. Maybe she'd still be alive."

His voice cracked and he looked down at his food, clearly struggling with his emotions. He looked up again finally. "So, I tried to be there for her, listen if she needed it. She was great at helping others but not so good at accepting it for herself, you know?"

Cindy nodded. Lots of people had that problem.

"Then, right around Christmas something changed," Beau said.

"What changed?"

"I don't know. It was like the light came back on inside her. She started laughing and smiling again. At the Christmas party she was just...glowing. That's the only way I can describe it. I didn't know what had changed, but I was so grateful that she was no longer mourning so deeply."

A smile touched his face as he remembered and it made Cindy's heart ache a little for him and for Rose.

"And then I didn't want to stress her out. It was like I was afraid that her happiness was this fragile bubble that might break if anything new or different touched it. I was an idiot," he said.

"Sometimes we're too afraid of how things might change if we do speak up, even if the change could be a good one," she said.

Heaven knew it had taken her and Jeremiah both a long time to speak up about their feelings for each other. Too long. She sometimes wondered how things would be different if they'd only worked that out sooner.

She took a deep breath. This was so not about them. She stared intently at Beau. The man was in anguish. She wished there was something she could do to help him. Impulsively she reached across the table and touched his arm.

"Beau, I promise you I'll find out what happened to her," she said.

Tears welled in his eyes. "Thank you," he said. "If she's alive I need to find her, to tell her what I should have told her months ago. And if she's not..." he shuddered. "If she's not, I need to know that, too," he finally finished.

"You will," she said, tears beginning to sting her eyes.

Beau glanced down for a moment and then stood up. "I have to go," he muttered.

He left and she set about eating her lunch. Her heart really did ache for him. When her lunch break was finally over she headed back to her floor. She stepped off the elevator and before she could turn and head for her desk Mr. Cartwright loomed over her, his face contorted in menace.

"What do you think you are doing?" he demanded.

16

Cindy nearly jumped out of her skin. "Heading to my desk," she finally managed to get out.

"Where have you been?"

"Lunch."

"You're late getting back."

"No, I took lunch late. I waited all morning for you and finally gave up," she said, not wanting to tell him she'd been hoping to catch Beau at lunch.

He stared at her sourly, but didn't say anything.

"I've been creating a filing system for all the papers I've found on the desk and in the desk. Apparently my predecessor didn't have one," Cindy finally said, feeling the need to break the silence that was stretching between them.

If anything his glower got worse. "Keep doing that. And be ready tomorrow morning for a lot of hard work."

"Okay," she said.

"I'll be in my office," he said.

"Alright."

He turned and went into his office, slamming the door. She jumped slightly.

What a horrible, horrible man, she thought to herself before turning and making her way back to her desk.

"Mr. Cartwright seems to be in a bad mood," she commented to Leo, needing to say something to someone.

"He often is," Leo said dully.

"I wonder why he was so late getting in."

"Boss's privilege," he said. "The rest of us have to suck it up and get to work on time no matter how hard our heads are pounding. He can just sleep it off."

"Was he at the bachelor party, too?" Cindy asked sharply.

Leo turned to look at her. "Of course he was. It was his bachelor party."

"Oh!"

"Yeah, he's getting married this weekend. I'm telling you he planned all that out just right. He'll be set for life."

"What do you mean?"

Leo yawned. "He's marrying Nita Rayburn."

"Rayburn? As in this company? Rayburn NextGen Solutions?"

"Yup, owner's daughter. One day, all of this will be his," he said, sweeping his hand around to indicate the whole place. "As long as he doesn't screw things up."

"Is he likely to? I mean, screw things up?"

"Not unless he's stupid. Apparently he used to like to date...a lot...but ever since Nita he's kept his eyes on the prize. Least, that's what the best man was saying last night. I think. That sounds right, right?"

"Um, I guess so. He must have finally found a woman he could love."

Leo snorted. "Yeah, sure."

"You don't think he loves her?"

"Oh, I'm sure he loves her. My great uncle used to say it was just as easy to fall in love with a rich woman as a poor woman. And he was married five times."

"Sounds like a real winner," Cindy said, unable to hide

her disgust.

"I don't know. He must be doing something right. He's sitting on a beach in Aruba sucking up martinis and I'm stuck here doing mindless work that I could do in my sleep," Leo said.

"Well, at least you have friends, like Mr. Cartwright."

Leo laughed again. "He's not my friend."

"Then why did you go to his party?"

"They needed bodies. I think I got invited because I worked on the same floor. He can hold a grudge, I'll tell you, so I figured it would be bad for my career if I didn't go. I'm just grateful he didn't ask me to be a groomsman."

"He must have some friends then."

"The best man. They went to college together. Real piece of work. I think they were in the Alpha Sigma Sigma fraternity together."

Cindy shook her head, not knowing what that was.

"You know... A-S-S."

"Oh," she said with a short embarrassed chuckle. Leo was clearly still hung over and Cindy doubted she would have gotten this much information out of him if that hadn't been the case. He rubbed his head, clearly feeling the effects still.

"How much did you drink last night?" she asked before she could stop herself.

He turned to look at her. "I don't know. Two beers is my limit. I remember starting on the second beer and not much else after that. I can't figure out what went wrong."

"Maybe you didn't hydrate enough or eat enough?" Cindy guessed. She'd heard those things could make alcohol go to your head faster.

"Whatever it was, I don't want to look at another beer

again as long as I live."

"Seriously?"

"Probably not. It just feels like that at the moment."
Cindy smiled.

Leo turned back to his computer. She should get back to
work, too. Her foot brushed against the box with Rose's
stuff in it and she thought about taking it into Mr.
Cartwright's office. Given the force with which he'd
slammed the door, though, and his seeming desire not to
see her until the morning she decided it could wait.
Besides, she might still find a few things crammed in
between all the other papers that should go in the box.

*And it has nothing to do with the fact that I don't want
to have to interact with him again today...right*, she thought
rolling her eyes at herself.

~

Mark had thought carefully about what Jeremiah told
him after he left the hospital. If it was true that one of the
officers who had gone to Rebecca's shop knew Mason then
he needed to move quickly and carefully. It only took a
phone call to discover that the Bobbsey twins had been on
scene. Lou and Frances were two peas in a pod. They
talked in similar ways and even looked a lot alike, which
explained some of Rebecca's confusion. She wouldn't be
the first person to mistake one for the other.

Lou he'd known for several years. Frances had joined
the department a little less than two years earlier. All Mark
really knew about him was that he had a weird sense of
humor. If one of the two was actually friends with Mason,
his money would be on Frances. It could easily be a

misunderstanding, though. Frances had an odd sense of humor. Rebecca wouldn't be the first victim Mark would have to explain that to.

Of course, there had been two active crime scenes within mere feet of each other, one being her shop and the other being the sidewalk where Liam was attacked. It was possible that one of the other officers from outside had come into the shop and made those comments to her and that it hadn't been either Lou or Frances. A lot of officers had been through that area yesterday. There were only a couple he knew for sure had been nowhere near it.

He felt bad about doing it but the next thing he did was call Taylor at home.

"Detective, what can I do for you?" the man asked hesitantly.

"I'm just checking in on you."

"I haven't changed my mind about quitting yet, if that's what you're asking. However, I am taking a few days off to think about it like you suggested," he said.

"And I'm glad you're taking my advice," Mark said, wincing slightly. "But, I need your help with something."

"What?" Taylor asked.

"I need you to discretely make some phone calls and see if you can find a Mason Dunwoody in the area. He's former special forces. I can pull up his file and I can send you what I have."

There was a pause. Then Taylor asked, "Why are you coming to me with this?"

"Because there is a remote possibility that someone on the force knows him and I don't want to show my hand too soon if that's the case. Can you do this for me?"

There was an awkward pause before Taylor said, "I

don't think I'm the man for the job."

"See, I think you're the perfect man for the job. And it's important. This Mason guy is stalking Liam's girlfriend."

"Is he the one who put Liam in the hospital yesterday?"

"He's my lead suspect. I just need to find out if he's in the area," Mark said.

"Okay."

"Thanks, Taylor. I'll send you information shortly."

As it turned out Mason had been arrested a couple of times for battery when he was younger. There was nothing since he'd left the military, but he might have just gotten better at hiding his tracks or intimidating his victims. Mark sent what he had to Taylor before leaving the precinct.

Hopefully Taylor would find Mason so they could deal with this whole mess quickly. Helping save a fellow officer and a young lady might also make Taylor rethink his decision to quit the force. Sometimes cops just needed to be reminded of all the good they did, including him.

As much as possible he tried to clear his head as he drove over to Ruth's house to see her and Casey. Liam's attacker wasn't the only mystery he needed to solve. After getting some sleep he was more convinced than ever that Casey couldn't have killed their parents. If he could get him to open up, though, it might be that Casey could tell him some vital information that might help Mark figure out who the real killer was.

Ruth lived in a duplex in a less affluent section of town than he would have expected. She welcomed him inside. Casey was sitting on an old sofa playing with an iPad. Mark gingerly sat down on the other end of the sofa and watched him for a minute.

Ruth sat down on a chair close to Mark, nervously

smoothing down her skirt.

"How are you doing?" he asked.

"I don't know. He kept waking up in the middle of the night with nightmares. He's quiet now, but... Sometimes I don't know what he's thinking or feeling. Obviously he's upset, but then he'll get distracted and it's like nothing is wrong..." she drifted off.

"Okay, but that's not what I asked," Mark said gently. "I asked how you are doing?"

She looked at him, clearly startled. "No one ever asks how I'm doing," she whispered as though compelled to say it.

"I'm sorry," he said, trying to put as much sympathy into his voice as he could. "How are you doing?"

"I want to scream. Like a lot," she said, biting her lip and looking away.

"It's understandable. You lost both your parents. I'm hoping you can put all the horror behind you soon and just remember the good times, the love," he said.

He hated trying to give grief counseling. He always felt useless, like he didn't know what to say. Unfortunately, it was part of the job sometimes. He just babbled a bit hoping that whatever he said would be the right thing.

From the way that Ruth's face was hardening, though, he suddenly realized that he must have said something wrong.

"Love?" she asked, eyes blazing. "Love? You know what my parents loved?"

"You and your brother?" he said even though he realized he should have kept his mouth shut.

"No! That bat! That stupid, ridiculous bat!"

"They loved the bat," Mark asked quietly.

"Yes! More than their own children. Certainly more than me. Look at this place! They wouldn't have let the bat live in squalor like this."

"It doesn't seem fair," Mark said, senses alive as he watched her like a hawk.

"No! All my life they've showed it off like their most cherished possession."

"That should have been you," he said.

"Of course it should have been me! Then he came along..." she said, turning to glare at her brother.

"And it was all about him and the bat, wasn't it?"

"Yes!"

"They took you for granted. They didn't give you the love and attention you deserved," Mark continued.

"That's right! It was always the same."

"But you got what you deserved, didn't you?" Mark asked, holding his breath as he pushed slightly.

"I did! That bat was mine, my inheritance."

"It just came to you a little early."

"Yes, and I was so glad when it was gone," Ruth ranted, her face red and swollen, her eyes darting crazily around the room.

"And the money you got for it was going to make your life so much better, was going to be them giving you what you deserved, wasn't it?"

"Yes!"

"And they would never know that you replaced it with another bat. It looked just the same. What did it matter?"

"They made me stare at that signature so many times! I knew how to write it better than my own name!" she shouted.

She was overwrought, but she had just admitted to

stealing the bat

"But then something awful happened," Mark guessed. "The bat that was always locked up in its display case was about to come out of it."

"They wanted to loan it to a six month traveling exhibit! Can you imagine?"

"That meant having it reassessed for insurance purposes. That would have been unthinkable," Mark said.

"Two decades it sat in that case and suddenly they wanted to take it out!"

"You had to do something," Mark said.

"I did."

"If it looked like a burglar broke in and stole it then everything would end up just fine."

"And it would have been fine," Ruth said.

The anger was giving way to grief and horror. He had seen it happen before and he waited for the confession he knew was coming.

"But then they came home early. They were supposed to be gone all day. All of a sudden I heard them come in the front door, and then they were in the kitchen."

"You were trapped."

Ruth was crying now. "And they stayed there and they kept talking and talking and they were talking about the stupid bat. About how much it meant to them."

"It was too much."

"I hit dad first and then mom. I just wanted to knock them out, so they wouldn't see me, and so they'd stop talking. They fell, and the bat was covered in..."

She started sobbing.

"What did you do then?"

"I dropped it...and...and I called...911."

"And then you left?" he asked.

She nodded.

"But when you came back later, after you cleaned up, you realized something else had gone wrong."

"Casey," she said with a gasp. "He was supposed to be next door at the neighbor's house. They watched him on Tuesdays. He would play with their dogs."

"He came back and found them. And they weren't just knocked out."

She collapsed completely then. Casey looked up finally from his iPad, his face contorting in fear.

"It's going to be alright," he told Casey as he pulled his phone out of his pocket.

It was a lie, but he didn't know what else to say.

17

Cindy was feeling distinctly unsettled. The work day was winding down and she'd made considerable progress on getting the papers filed. One thing she had noticed was that none of them seemed to predate October. She knew from Beau that Rose had worked at the company longer than that, but that her grandmother had died in October.

It made her wonder where all the files from before that were. It was possible Rose had kept them somewhere else and that as she was dealing with her grief she just let the unfiled papers pile up.

She decided that in the morning after her meeting with Mr. Cartwright she'd try to find if there were filing cabinets that Rose might have been using prior to October.

Even though she'd only found a couple more personal things within the papers it still felt morbid, going through someone else's stuff. Especially when she was half-convinced that something bad had happened to that person.

A sudden horrible memory that she'd done her best for years to forget suddenly bubbled to the surface. Her mom had taken her into Lisa's room, a few weeks after she had died. Cindy had been forced to go through her sister's things, deciding what to keep, what to get rid of. Her mom had refused to help with the job, just sent Cindy in and told her to get it done.

Her chest tightened at the memory of it. She'd gone

through her sister's clothes, bagging them all for Goodwill. The thought of keeping any of them had made her physically ill. Then she'd gone through Lisa's toys and stuffed animals, most of which were already boxed up in her closet. She'd kept a few for her mother and Kyle. The rest she'd put in another trash bag for Goodwill.

After that she'd gone through her sister's jewelry box. She tried to choose something for herself to keep, to remember Lisa by. In the end she couldn't do it, though. Every single piece reminded her too deeply of her sister and the pain that brought reduced her to tears.

That tiny jewelry box and its contents were in a box in the bottom of the closet of Geanie's old bedroom at her house. She'd never brought herself to look at any of it again after that day. Neither had she been able to throw it away, though.

The worst part, though, had been having to go through Lisa's books and papers. Cindy had found the secret diary her sister kept. She'd only read the first couple of pages, enough to see her sister's thoughts on life, her parents, their family. She decided that those were the thoughts her sister hadn't wanted to share in life, so why should she be forced to in death? Cindy had destroyed the book.

Tears began to roll down her cheeks and she hunched over as she tried to wipe them away. She didn't want anyone to glance over and see her. The half walls that afforded only limited privacy now made her feel like she had been exposed for all the world to see, her soul laid bare.

It was almost too much for her.

How on earth did Rose cope with this?

If she was grieving the death of the woman who had

raised her then Rose must have shed many tears at this desk. Who would have seen, noticed? Who would have tried to bring her comfort?

Cindy felt her heart begin to race. Who indeed?

Beau had said a change came over Rose just before Christmas. She became happier, glowing even. She thought about the picture of Rose sitting on Santa's lap. She looked like a woman in love.

Who comforted you, Rose? she whispered the words out loud.

She swiveled her chair around, forgetting about her own embarrassment over crying at her desk.

"Leo, did you go to the company Christmas party a few months ago?" she asked.

He looked up. His eyes looked dull and he still looked quite the worse for wear. "Um, yeah, why?"

She bit her lip. "Do you know who was playing Santa Claus?" she asked.

"Sure. Every year Mr. Rayburn chooses one of the executives to play Santa at the party. This past Christmas it was Mr. Cartwright."

~

There were days Mark really hated his job and this was one of them. While it was a relief to have a killer in custody, he was deeply saddened that was Ruth. She hadn't gone to her parents' house that morning planning to kill them. She hadn't planned on seeing them. Now with their parents dead and his sister going to jail for their murder, Casey had no one.

Casey's doctor was with him and a man from Protective

Services trying to sort out where Casey was going to go. Apparently there were some cousins that were a possibility. The older couple who lived next door and watched him once a week had even come forward to express their willingness to take the young man in.

Although he was hoping for the best there was no telling how long Ruth would be in jail. Once she was out she wouldn't be able to get custody of Casey, but maybe they could start to rebuild a little of what they'd lost. At least, he liked to think so. The reality, though, was that there was no hopeful future for that sibling relationship.

He still wasn't sure whether it had been Ruth's idea or her lawyer's to go ahead and let Casey take the fall for the murders. That was the part of this whole mess that irked him the most. Casey had been able to tell him and the doctor that Ruth had said if he was willing to go to a hospital that she could visit him and they'd still be together.

It was unclear to Mark if Casey knew that his sister had murdered their parents or not. Either way, it wasn't his job to make sure he understood. Heck, if it were up to him he'd never tell the kid that his sister was the cause of the whole mess.

His phone rang and he grabbed it from his pocket. It was Traci.

"Hello?" he answered.

"Hi, hon. I'm just checking up on you," Traci said in her perkiest voice.

"Is something wrong?" he asked, sitting up straight.

"Not with me. Is something wrong with you?" she asked.

"I...no, I mean, rough day. Why do you ask?"

"I just got this feeling that I should call you and make sure you're handling all the dirty work okay."

"It's dirtier than usual, but I'm hanging in there," he said.

"I'm making my lasagna for dinner."

"Wait, do you mean the frozen lasagna you get at the store or your actual lasagna?"

"My actual made-from-scratch recipe," she informed him proudly.

"Oh, man, you haven't made that in months and months," he said, feeling himself already beginning to salivate at the prospect.

"Not since before we got pregnant," she confirmed.

"How long until it comes out of the oven?"

"An hour."

"I will be there," he vowed. "I don't care what happens where in the universe tonight, I'm going to have some of that lasagna straight out of the oven."

"It's true, the way to a man's heart is through his stomach. Or, rather, his taste buds in this case," Traci said, sounding quite smug.

"You laugh now, but just you wait until I eat all the lasagna by myself and don't leave you a single piece."

"Oh, I see how it is. You want to engage in smack talk now?"

"I thought it might be appropriate."

He couldn't help but chuckle at that.

"Listen, Mark, I'm sorry. I shouldn't have pushed you yesterday on the phone."

"No, you were right to do so," he said. "I've been holding onto Pa- er, the past far too long," he said, changing his phrasing at the last moment because he was not going to mention Paul's name in the precinct. "It's time I got whatever other answers I can and just let go."

"You know I'm here for you."

"You always are, and I don't think I thank you often enough for that."

"You're cute," she said, and he could tell she was grinning.

"If you think I'm cute now, wait until you see me attack that lasagna," he said.

She started giggling and it warmed him up inside. The evils of the world seemed to melt away as he concentrated on that laugh. He closed his eyes and let it envelop him.

"I love you," she finally said.

"I love you, too. I'll be home in time for lasagna."

"You better," she teased.

After she hung up he called Taylor. It went to the man's voicemail and Mark left a message. Then he tried calling Jeremiah's phone, but it also went to voicemail.

"You know what they say, no news is good news," he muttered to himself.

~

"Help!" Jeremiah shouted at the top of his lungs.

Beneath him Rebecca was convulsing, her body going into shock. He was laying across her legs and pinning her right shoulder with his left hand as he held a fistful of hospital sheets down on the stab wound in her abdomen that was gushing blood.

"Nurse! Emergency!" he shouted again. "Woman's been stabbed!"

He heard a commotion as several people arrived in the

room at once. He glanced up for a fraction of a second and saw a young, female doctor, two nurses, one man and one woman, and the police officer who hadn't been at his guard post moments before.

He heard the doctor exclaim.

"Help me! She's been stabbed and she's losing blood fast!" he screamed, praying that they could understand him. He could hear his voice and his accent was thicker, brought out by the stress of the moment and his need to communicate quickly.

"Get a gurney!" the doctor ordered the male nurse.

The man bolted from the room.

"When did this happen?" the doctor barked.

"Couldn't have been more than a minute ago," Jeremiah said, trying to enunciate clearly.

Rebecca was still fighting him and he was struggling to keep hold of her. She was laying diagonally across Liam's hospital bed, with Liam underneath her. Why he wasn't waking up Jeremiah didn't know. He should have with the weight and the noise and all the thrashing about. He should be awake and screaming in pain and fear.

But he wasn't.

And the way they were rolling about on top of him there was a very real chance that one of his damaged organs could take a fatal blow. For all their sakes he needed to get Rebecca off of Liam.

The nurse came sprinting back in with the gurney. It slammed against the one wall before he could turn it. The other nurse scrambled to help him and they got it into position on the other side of the hospital bed toward the foot. Jeremiah looked across at them and saw something out of the corner of his eye that sent chills through him.

The IV bag that Liam was hooked up to had been full of clear liquids since he got into the room after surgery. Now, though, there was pale green liquid swirling around in it.

With a shout Jeremiah let go of Rebecca's shoulder and lunged further across her to grab hold of the tubing leading from the bag to the IV in Liam's hand. He bent it, stopping the flow of liquid.

"What are you doing?" the doctor shouted.

"That's not his medication," Jeremiah grunted.

She turned wide eyes to the bag. She reached up and shut off the drip. "Get off her, we have to transfer her," she snapped as she turned back.

Jeremiah slithered back as far as he could. His feet had a precarious purchase on the floor which was slippery from the coffee he'd spilled moments ago. In order to stand up far enough so they could move her onto the gurney he was going to have to let go of the wound.

"1, 2, 3," he said.

He jumped back, grabbed her knees and helped the other two nurses lift her free of the hospital bed and onto the gurney. The female nurse put pressure back down on the wound as the doctor grabbed the foot of the gurney.

"Operating room, now!" the doctor shouted as the male nurse began to back out of the room pulling the gurney.

He wanted to go with them. He took a step forward and then turned to look at Liam. "Send in another doctor! We don't know what he's been dosed with!" Jeremiah shouted.

"I need a team in that room now!" he heard the doctor roar as they made it into the hall with the gurney.

He could hear feet scrambling, alarms blaring, someone speaking over a PA System paging specific doctors by name.

He glanced again at Liam. There was blood on him, but Jeremiah was relatively sure it was Rebecca's.

He turned toward the police officer who was just standing there, gaping at Liam. Jeremiah took three strides forward, grabbed the man by the throat, and slammed him into the wall.

"Where were you?" he growled.

18

The police officer was clawing at Jeremiah's hand around his throat, but to no avail. The man should have instead tried to jab Jeremiah in the eyes or the throat, but he didn't have his wits about him enough to do it.

"I asked you a question," Jeremiah hissed. "Where were you?"

The man's eyes bugged out of his head as he gasped for breath and clawed more frantically at Jeremiah's hand. Jeremiah loosened his grip just enough so the man could get words out.

"The nurse's station. I was just gone for a minute."

A minute was all it had taken.

Jeremiah had arrived at the hospital ten minutes earlier. He'd checked in with Rebecca and then went downstairs to get both of them some coffee. When he had left the room the officer had been sitting in his chair. When he came back with the coffee the officer had been gone.

He'd rushed inside, seen Rebecca laying diagonally across Liam with the blood pumping out of her stomach wound. He dropped the coffee and leaped instantly on top of her to try and staunch the flow of blood and to restrict her movements.

He heard running footsteps and a startled oath.

"Sir, let the police officer go," a shaky voice said moments later.

Jeremiah turned and saw a doctor standing there, wearing scrubs, gloves, and a mask. He looked like he'd been just prepped for surgery.

Jeremiah released the officer and stepped back. He would finish dealing with him afterward.

"A foreign substance was introduced into this IV bag," Jeremiah said, moving over to indicate it. "I don't know if it's a paralytic, some sort of poison, or what. There has to be some already in his system given that he didn't wake up a minute ago."

The doctor gaped from him to the IV bag.

"Let's go!" Jeremiah boomed, his voice filling the room.

The doctor scrambled forward and unhooked the bag. He handed it to a nurse who had followed him in. "Take this to the lab, give it to Sergei for testing. Tell him it's an emergency."

The woman nodded, grabbed the bag, and dashed from the room. The doctor grabbed Liam's chart with hands that had started to shake. He skimmed through it then put it down and approached Liam. "Bring me a light," he barked.

Another nurse scrambled forward with a penlight. They pried open one of Liam's eyelids and shone the light in his eye. Then he yanked a stethoscope out of the nurse's hands and listened to Liam's heart and lungs.

"What exactly happened in here?" the man asked, turning to Jeremiah.

Jeremiah told him what he knew.

"Alright, we need to get this man to imaging right now to check on his liver and spleen, make sure they didn't sustain any more damage."

"What do you think he was dosed with?" Jeremiah

asked.

"No idea yet. Hopefully he was just put under."

"And how soon will you know?"

The doctor shook his head then turned to his nurses. "Alright, let's get him out of here. Everyone move."

They took the brakes off the bed Liam was in which was just another glorified gurney. They then started to wheel him out.

"Stay here so I know where to find you," the doctor instructed Jeremiah.

He nodded.

The doctor and nurses left and Jeremiah and the officer were once again alone. The other man was struggling to pull himself together. He glared at Jeremiah. "I know you're friends with the detectives, but you've just committed battery against a police officer. You know what kind of sentence that carries?"

Jeremiah stepped close to the other man and dropped his voice low. "Yeah, a lot shorter one than killing a police officer. Of course, they'd never be able to prove either."

The man's eyes widened in terror and he reached for his gun. Jeremiah grabbed it before he could and shoved it into his waistband. He locked his eyes on the other man. "Now, you're going to tell me everything that happened after I left this room a few minutes ago."

~

Cindy was tired as she headed to Liam's room in the hospital. Jeremiah had left her a voicemail saying he'd meet her there after work. Her mind was still spinning with the thought that something had happened between Rose and Mr. Cartwright.

She could hear someone speaking over the PA system. They were speaking rapidly but whatever they were saying was too garbled for her to understand. She reached Liam's room, walked in and stopped dead in her tracks as she saw Jeremiah slap a police officer.

"What is going on?" she asked, bewildered.

"That's what I'm trying to find out," Jeremiah growled.

She stared at the two men and pulled her phone out of her purse. Mark picked up on the second ring.

"Cindy, is everything okay?"

"Um, I'm not sure. I just arrived at Liam's room. Neither he nor Rebecca is here but Jeremiah is...questioning...a police officer."

"Questioning?"

"Yes. Aggressively," Cindy added.

There was a torrent of what sounded like profanity from Mark. Fortunately he slurred it together so much that she only caught a couple of words in all of it, most notably 'lasagna'. There was a pause and then he hung up.

She wasn't sure exactly what that meant but she returned her phone to her purse.

"Where's Liam?" she asked.

"Getting x-rays," Jeremiah said.

"And Rebecca?"

"Being operated on."

"What?" she asked, feeling like she'd just stepped into some episode of The Twilight Zone where nothing was making any sense.

"She was stabbed and Liam poisoned while this gentleman wasn't at his post," Jeremiah said, his voice steely.

"Oh!" Cindy exclaimed.

"Now I'm going to find out why he wasn't doing his job."

"I told you, I was at the nurse's station," the man said. He had turned a sickly gray color and was sweating profusely.

"Why?"

"They said I had a call."

"Who from?" Jeremiah demanded.

"I don't know. The nurse who told me didn't give me a name. When I picked up the phone no one was there."

"That should have taken all of twenty seconds," Jeremiah said.

"Yeah, well I asked the nurses who had been calling since I figured it had to be important. They were trying to find the woman who had answered the phone in the first place. So, while I waited I called the precinct to make sure no one there was trying to get hold of me. By the time the nurse who answered the phone could talk to me probably four or five minutes had passed. Tops."

"And what did that nurse say?"

"Just that it was a man and that he hadn't left a name, just that it was urgent that he speak to the officer guarding Liam O'Neill's room."

"It sounds like someone was trying to draw him away," Cindy interjected.

"Maybe. Or maybe someone paid him to leave his post," Jeremiah said.

She stared at him. He was acting paranoid. There had to be more going on than she was aware of. "What exactly did happen?" she asked.

"While he was gone, someone came in and put a foreign

substance into Liam's IV drip. They then stabbed Rebecca. I found her almost immediately after that. She was in no condition to say anything about what had happened, unfortunately."

"Their attacker could still be in the building," Cindy said.

"Not likely. He had plenty of time to escape while I was getting help."

"Okay, if we can't catch him right now and the doctors are working with Liam and Rebecca, let's all take a deep breath, sit down, and figure out what happened," Cindy said.

To her relief, Jeremiah gave a short nod and took a step back from the police officer. He grabbed a chair and indicated that the other man should take one, too. After they were both sitting Cindy collapsed into a chair.

"Step me through it," she said.

Jeremiah settled farther into his chair and the look of agitation left his face. What remained was his customary neutral expression. She was always impressed when he could do that. Sometimes she was also a little irritated. It could be a weird experience discussing something with someone who was refusing to emote.

"I got here at a quarter past five. I came in and said hello to Rebecca. Liam was sleeping. I asked her if I could get her something. She requested coffee. I left and went down to the cafeteria where I was for five minutes. When I left the room, he was sitting in the chair outside," Jeremiah said, indicating the officer.

"About thirty seconds after I saw him leave, a nurse came up to me and told me I had a phone call at the nurses' station. I went to answer it and discovered that there was no one on the end of the line. I asked the two nurses who were there if they knew who had called me. They didn't and they said they hadn't answered the phone. I told them it was important that I find out who had been trying to reach me. The one went to go find whoever answered the phone. While she was gone I called the precinct on my cell just to make sure no one there had tried calling. They hadn't. It took a few minutes but the nurse who had answered the phone came and told me that it had been a male caller who didn't identify himself. He asked to speak with the officer on duty, so he didn't have my name. As soon as she finished telling me that I heard shouting. I ran to the room."

"Where I was trying to staunch the flow of blood from Rebecca's wound," Jeremiah said. "I'd made it back into the room about ten seconds before that. He wasn't sitting in the chair."

"Because I was at the nurses' station," the officer growled. "Like I said."

"What did you see when you came into the room?" Cindy asked Jeremiah.

"Rebecca was lying on her back diagonally across Liam and the hospital bed. Blood was gushing from a stab wound in her abdomen. I dropped the coffee, lunged on top of her and tried to stop her from thrashing around as I put pressure on the wound. I yelled for help. As it arrived I noticed the foreign substance in Liam's IV, a pale green liquid, and I put a crimp in the tube until the doctor could turn off the drip."

"Okay, that's weird," Cindy said, trying to puzzle it all out. She turned back to the police officer. "Did you see anything at all when you were at the nurses' station, glance back at the room?"

The officer frowned in thought for a moment. "I did see a nurse go into the room, I think."

"Male or female?" Cindy asked.

"Male. I think he came in here. I just got a quick glimpse."

Cindy exchanged glances with Jeremiah. That could have been Rebecca's stalker.

"Something is bothering me," Cindy said.

"What?"

"If he had a knife, why bother putting something in Liam's IV?" she asked. "Why didn't he just stab him?"

"That's a good question," Jeremiah said with a frown. "Maybe the knife was just a backup and Rebecca figured out what was going on before he could get out of there."

"If he's obsessed with her why stab her?" she asked.

The police officer jumped in. "That's not that unheard of. He gets angry that she's with the other guy or he realizes she's never going to come back to him, and he just snaps and attacks her."

"If that was the plan all along, though, why stab one and not the other?" Cindy questioned. "It's inefficient."

"Maybe stabbing her wasn't part of the plan. Maybe he was hoping to come in, tamper with the IV, and get out before anyone could figure out what he'd done," Jeremiah said.

"Wouldn't he realize she would recognize him?" Cindy asked.

"He could have disguised his features some."

"I guess," Cindy mused. "We're probably not going to know until Rebecca is out of surgery and she can tell us exactly what happened."

Jeremiah grimaced. "There's a good chance she's not going to make it," he said quietly.

"Then we need to pray," Cindy said.

"I've been doing that already," he said.

"Pray harder."

He nodded his head.

Even though her mind was racing Cindy managed to pray for Rebecca and Liam and the doctors working on them.

Suddenly she heard running steps. She twisted around to see the door just as Mark burst through it. His hair was standing on end, his tie was askew, and his eyes were blazing with a feverish madness. He looked around the room, noticed the missing bed, and opened his mouth in a silent snarl. Then he strode straight up to Jeremiah and glared at him.

A torrent of words issued from Mark's mouth, none of them recognizable except for the last one.

"Lasagna!"

19

"Mark, are you speaking in tongues?" Cindy asked, sounding bewildered.

The comment surprised Jeremiah and he struggled not to laugh out loud at it. The detective had indeed seemed to be speaking pure gibberish.

A vein in Mark's forehead was throbbing. He glared at all three of them. "Tell me why I'm not home eating lasagna," he growled.

It only took a couple of minutes to bring him up to speed. At the end Jeremiah thought Mark was going to take a swing at the officer, too.

Mark's phone rang and after glaring at the officer he went outside to answer it. A minute later he came back glowering harder. "No luck yet on finding the guy we're looking for," he said.

Silence descended as each of them realized there was nothing to do now but wait. Mark finally sat down in a chair and he looked defeated. He glanced up at the police officer. "Go home and get some rest."

"My shift isn't up for another hour," the man protested.

"There's no one here to guard. If there is before your relief gets here I'll handle it," Mark said.

The officer looked at Jeremiah. Jeremiah smiled slowly at him, putting just enough menace into it to hopefully scare him enough to go away and not make a nuisance of himself.

The man winced and left the room without another word.

"What did you do to him?" Mark asked after the man had gone.

"Do you really want to know?" Jeremiah asked.

"No."

"You should go home, too," Cindy told Mark gently.

"No, I'm good."

"Go home, Mark. Traci and the lasagna are waiting. We have no idea how long it will be before we hear anything here. Once we do I'll call," Jeremiah said.

"You had me at lasagna," Mark said as he stood up. "Just do me a favor."

"What?"

"Don't hurt the next officer who comes on duty."

"You know I can't make a promise like that. I don't know who they are."

Mark hung his head in defeat. "Call."

"We will," Cindy said.

Mark left the room and it was just Cindy and him. She glanced over at him. "Are you okay?"

"Not really," he admitted.

"Do you want me to go get you a shirt so you can clean up?" she asked.

He glanced down and realized that he was covered in Rebecca's blood. He hadn't noticed. "Yeah, that would probably be a good idea," he said with a sigh. He dug his keys out of his pocket and handed them to her. "I have a spare shirt in my trunk," he said.

"In case of emergencies like this?" she asked.

"In case of emergencies like this," he affirmed.

She smirked, but didn't say anything.

She got up and headed out of the room. He walked into the bathroom in the room and stripped off his bloody shirt. He dropped it in the trash. He began scrubbing his hands and arms vigorously with soap under the hot water.

Just as he was toweling off Cindy appeared with a clean white shirt in her hands. As she handed it to him she blushed slightly.

"You've seen me shirtless before," he said.

She nodded, biting her lip.

Suddenly he realized she was remembering their trip to Israel and the kiss they'd shared after the battle. He'd been shirtless then. He smiled. Death and carnage and what she focused on was the kiss.

That was good because he did, too.

He put on the clean shirt and then went back out and sat on one of the chairs. "Better?" he asked.

She just smiled. Her smile faded a moment later, though. "That was a lot of blood," she said.

"Yeah, it was."

"What do you think her chances are?"

"Not great, but we moved on it as soon as we possibly could."

"I feel so bad for them."

"I know, me, too."

Cindy's stomach growled. "I'm hungry," she admitted with a grimace.

"I can hold down the fort while you go get something to eat."

"Do you want me to bring you something to eat?" she asked.

"Yeah. And maybe a replacement coffee," he said,

noticing the cup that had rolled into the corner.

"I've got my phone," she said.

"Great."

Cindy left the room.

Where did Rebecca's phone go? Jeremiah suddenly wondered.

He got up and went over to the desk that she had been sitting at when he'd first showed up. Her purse was still there on the floor by her chair. The coded papers were still on the table. The phone, though, was not where it had been. When he left to get coffee the phone he'd given her was on the table.

He looked around the chair, then checked her purse to make sure it hadn't fallen in there. He swept the room. It wasn't there. Rebecca had been wearing leggings and a long-sleeve shirt. No pockets.

He grabbed his own phone out of his pocket. He'd put a tracker on the phone. He pulled up the information. The phone was currently about five miles away.

At Rebecca's shop.

He dialed Mark.

"Hello?"

"We've got him!" Jeremiah said. "He's at Rebecca's shop."

"How do you know?" Mark asked sharply.

"I realized the phone I gave Rebecca which was here before the attack is gone. I have a tracker on it."

"Don't you think he would have checked to see if there was one of those parental trackers on?" Mark asked.

"Not necessarily. He probably didn't expect anyone to notice for a while that the phone was missing. Plus, what I put on the phone he'd never find."

"I'm heading there right now. I'll call for backup."

"I'll meet you there," Jeremiah said, already moving out the door.

"No, we can handle it."

"He was special forces. If he's as scary as Rebecca thinks he is you're going to want me there."

"Okay, but don't go in without me."

Jeremiah ended the call. He was racing outside to his car now. He called Cindy, told her where he was going, and told her to wait back in the hospital room for word from the doctors. She clearly didn't like it, but she agreed.

A minute later he was speeding toward the shop. He glanced again at the tracker. It hadn't moved. It was possible Mason had gone there, ditched the phone, and left. That didn't make sense, though. As far as he knew both Rebecca and Liam were dead and no one was going to be looking for her phone for a while.

He had probably gone to her shop to connect with what had been hers or to grab a memento for himself.

Jeremiah turned onto the block where her shop was. Suddenly his phone rang. He expected the name to come up as Mark. Instead, it came up as Rebecca. Mason was calling him. His was one of only two numbers programmed into the phone so it made sense that Mason was trying to feel him out.

Jeremiah turned the wheel hard and slid into a parking space. He didn't want to drive up while on the phone and potentially give himself away.

"Hello?" he answered.

"Hello, Jeremiah," the voice on the other end was angry, but controlled.

"Who is this?" he asked.

"This is the man who just killed your girlfriend."

"Which one?" Jeremiah asked flippantly.

"Which one?" the man shouted, his control slipping.

"Yes, which girlfriend?"

"Rebecca!"

"Rebecca? I don't think...oh, Becky, are you talking about Becky?" Jeremiah asked.

He texted Mark that he had Mason talking on the phone and would do what he could to distract him. Hopefully it would help the police take him down. It wasn't how he had planned it, but this could work if he could rattle the guy enough.

"Her name is Rebecca! She hates being called Becky!"

"Not by me," Jeremiah purred.

"I'm going to kill you!"

A text from Mark popped up. *Keep him talking.*

Jeremiah chuckled. "And just how are you going to do that?"

"I'm going to gut you like a fish."

"You have to find me first. Who am I?"

"What?"

"I asked you a question, *Mason*," Jeremiah said, putting emphasis on the man's name. "Who am I?"

"You're one of Rebecca's lousy boyfriends."

"And beyond that?"

"What do you mean?" Mason growled.

"Who am I? What's my last name?"

"I don't know, but I'll find out."

Jeremiah chuckled again. "No, I don't think you will. That's okay. I know who you are."

"Oh yeah?"

"Yeah. You're Mason Dunwoody, former special

forces, psychopath, stalker, and all around bad boyfriend."

"I'm a great boyfriend!" Mason screamed.

"How could you be when you killed your girlfriend?"

There was a pause and then he heard what sounded like a muffled sob. "You don't understand, man. It's her and me. Forever."

"You know what? I'd be happy to send you to meet her," Jeremiah said, dropping his voice down.

"I'm going to-"

Jeremiah cut him off. "She died in my arms tonight. *My* arms. Not yours. If you wanted to be together, you missed your big chance. You failed. You couldn't even manage to kill yourself to be with her. There is no forever for you except forever apart."

Mason screamed incoherently into the phone. A second later there was a crash and he heard someone yell, "Freeze, police!"

Jeremiah sagged in relief. They had made it on time. A moment later he tensed up as he heard shots being fired.

He wrapped his hands around the steering wheel and squeezed. Willing himself to stay put. His sudden appearance on the scene would just add to the chaos and he couldn't trust the officers with Mark not to accidentally shoot him if he startled them.

There was another burst of noise over the phone and then he heard someone shouting, "Where'd he go?"

"No!" Jeremiah hissed, crushing the steering wheel tighter.

He glanced up the street toward the shop. He couldn't just sit by while Mason slipped through their fingers. He got out of the car quickly and quietly. He made his way down the street, keeping other cars and obstacles between himself and the shop as much as possible. He had no idea which way Mason had gone, but there was a clear exit up this way whereas the police cars seemed to have amassed at the other end of the street.

Finally he saw what he was looking for, a shadow running through the night. He was moving fast, but still being cautious, trying to choose a path that took him into the darkest patches of the street.

Jeremiah slid behind a car and crouched, waiting, watching as the man ran toward him. He couldn't see a weapon but that didn't mean Mason didn't have one.

At the last second Jeremiah stepped out of his hiding place and straight into Mason's path.

The man plowed to a stop just a couple of feet away. His eyes darted around Jeremiah and he coiled his muscles, clearly getting ready to try and lunge around him.

"Who am I?" Jeremiah asked.

Mason froze, a look of panic sweeping over his face. He was used to being the bully, used to taking others by surprise. It was clear that he couldn't take what he dished out.

"I know you don't know who I am," Jeremiah said with a smile. "Because if you did, you'd run."

20

Mark and the other officers exploded out of Rebecca's shop and scattered in different directions, searching for Mason. On a hunch Mark turned and ran up the street, wondering just how far away Jeremiah was.

He hadn't gone very far when two figures became visible in the darkness, about a block up. He poured on the speed. As he got close he could see that they were dancing around each other and he could hear the sound of a fist striking a body.

He recognized Jeremiah a second before the rabbi dropped the man he was fighting with. The way the other man fell it was clear he was unconscious before he hit the ground. Jeremiah dropped into a crouch over him and raised his fist.

"Don't kill him!" Mark shouted as he ran up.

Mark came to a stop in front of Jeremiah, panting slightly. He turned and looked at Mason who was out cold, limbs sprawled haphazardly on the ground.

He may have murdered my partner.

"I take it back. Go ahead and kill him," Mark growled.

"Sorry, too late," Jeremiah said, straightening up.

"What do you mean too late?" Mark asked.

"Three second rule."

"What is the three second rule?"

"The difference between self defense and murder."

"What on earth are you talking about?" Mark asked.

"Once my opponent goes unconscious it can take me up to three seconds to alter course. If I kill him within those three seconds it's just the conclusion of the fight. If I kill him after three seconds, it's an execution."

"There's nothing in the legal code about three seconds," Mark said.

"It's in *my* code," Jeremiah responded softly.

Mark kicked the man's arm lightly. "Oh look, he moved!"

Jeremiah narrowed his eyes. "I'm looking out for you."

"In what way?" Mark asked, his frustration nearly overwhelming him.

"If I kill him, I'll sleep fine. Will you?"

Mark cursed under his breath.

"See?"

He holstered his gun and got out his handcuffs which he quickly put on Mason. That done he stood and spoke into his radio. "Suspect is in custody. One block east of the shop."

"Get out of here. Call me when you know about Liam and Rebecca," he said.

Jeremiah nodded and seconds later was in his car driving away.

The first officers arrived about a minute later. "What happened to him?" one of them asked.

"A Good Samaritan," Mark said, unable to stop himself.

~

Cindy was relieved when Jeremiah made it back to the hospital just in time to watch an orderly wheel Liam back into the room. "It will take about an hour then the doctor will come in and explain all the test results to you," the man said.

"Thank you," Cindy said.

"Now we wait some more," Jeremiah said with a frustrated sigh as he took his seat once the orderly had left.

"Did you catch him?"

"We did," Jeremiah said.

"Did he confess?"

"Close enough. Have you had any word on Rebecca?"

Cindy shook her head. "No, and it's been pretty nerve wracking."

"I'm sorry," Jeremiah said.

"At least you got to do something helpful. I feel like the world's weirdest babysitter."

"It was important that someone was here in case either of them came back or the doctors needed to pass on information."

"Which was frightening in and of itself," Cindy said. "I don't know Rebecca. I mean, I know who she is, but I don't actually know her. I kept feeling like I should be calling her parents or siblings or something, but I don't even know if she has them. I don't know if she has an advanced medical directive. I don't know anything."

Her frustration was so overwhelming it almost brought her to tears. Jeremiah reached out and grabbed her hand. "It's okay," he said.

"Of course, I don't know that about Liam either. And I don't know how to contact his family and I don't know why he or Rebecca hasn't already. They should be here. Particularly if...if he dies," she forced herself to say.

"I know."

"But I don't," she said, all the fear and helplessness she'd been feeling for the last hour bubbled to the surface. "I don't know what I'm supposed to do if...if something happens to you."

Jeremiah frowned. "What do you mean?"

"I don't know what you want. Do you want to be kept on life support or not? What type of funeral do you want and where? How do I contact your family and let them know?"

"We have plenty of time to talk about that," he said.

"What if we don't?" she fired back. "Given our lives do you honestly think it couldn't just as easily be Liam and Rebecca sitting here while doctors were trying to figure out how to save us?"

Tears were now rolling down her cheeks. She tried to wipe them away with her free hand, but they just kept coming.

"Listen, you're tired, you're upset about everything that's going on. I promise you that we'll figure it all out later."

"When?"

"Soon."

He leaned forward and kissed her forehead. "Okay?"

She nodded even though she really wasn't.

A figure appeared in the door and Cindy felt a surge of anxiety flood through her. It was a doctor and the woman came quickly into the room. She glanced at Liam and then turned to them.

"How is Rebecca?" Jeremiah asked.

"Well, she's one tough cookie. She's in post-op now. We got her patched up and I think she's going to be okay."

Cindy felt a surge of relief. "When can we see her?"

"I've given instructions for her to be put in the room next door in about an hour or so when they move her."

"What about Liam?" Jeremiah asked.

"I haven't had a chance to look at any of his test results. I'm going to go do that and I'll be back when I have some answers."

"Thank you," Cindy said.

The doctor turned to leave then paused at the door. "They're very lucky to have you as friends, you know," she said over her shoulder.

"Are you going to call Mark?" Cindy asked.

"Yes," Jeremiah said, already pulling his phone out of his pocket.

Cindy listened as he relayed the message. She was tired, deep down bone tired. She'd been through a lot of crises, spent a lot of time in hospitals watching and praying and waiting. This felt different.

Maybe it was because in the morning she was going to have to go back to a job she hated. Maybe the fact that there was nothing for her to do, no way to help or figure things out was draining her faster. Whatever it was, she had an overwhelming urge to climb into bed, pull the covers over her head, and not come out for a week.

She glanced at the clock on the wall.

"Only thirty-six hours," she said.

"For what?" Jeremiah asked as he pocketed his phone.

"That's how long this has been going on," she said, indicating Liam and the hospital room. "That's fast in the scheme of things and yet it seems like it's taken forever."

"I'm tired, too," he said softly.

"It's more than just tired. It's, I don't know, unsettled," she said.

"Well, there is a lot that is currently unsettled."

"I guess. I'm just, I don't know...I feel like the ground underneath me keeps shifting and I don't know what to expect."

Jeremiah reached out and took her hand. "You can expect that I will always be here to catch you."

She squeezed his hand hard.

They sat in silence for what seemed like hours but in reality was only about thirty minutes. Then the doctor finally returned. Cindy almost leaped to her feet at the appearance. She realized her muscles had been coiled the entire time, waiting for the next thing to happen.

"I have some good news," the woman said, smiling slightly.

"We could use it," Cindy said.

"The foreign agent introduced into the IV bag would have killed him, but thanks to your quick thinking," she said, looking at Jeremiah, "only a small amount made it into his system. It was just enough to knock him out."

"Thank you, God," Cindy blurted out her prayer.

"What about his organs?" Jeremiah asked.

"It doesn't look like there was any additional damage done."

Cindy slumped in her chair.

"Is there still a chance one of them can rupture anyway?" Jeremiah asked.

"There is, but every hour that passes the odds get better that he's going to be just fine," the doctor said. "So, hopefully, if we can avoid any more excitement..."

"We'll do our best," Jeremiah said.

The doctor nodded. "I'll let you know when Rebecca is out of recovery and next door."

"Thank you," Cindy said.

"You should go home and get some rest," Jeremiah said after the doctor had left.

"I'm okay."

"No, you're not. You're exhausted and you've got work in the morning."

"So do you," she said.

"Actually no, tomorrow's Thursday. It's my day off," he said.

"That's right. Starting work on a Tuesday can really mess you up," she said. "Half the time I don't know what day it is."

"I know."

She sighed. "I wish I could take tomorrow off and spend it with you."

"Call in sick."

"It's a temp job, and a precarious one at that. Unless I'm throwing up or coughing up a lung or something I should go."

"You know, if you need to go into work and throw up on command you-"

Cindy held up a hand and wrinkled her nose. "I don't want to know."

Jeremiah shrugged.

"I'd hate to leave you here, by yourself," she said.

"The danger's past. I won't stay too late, I promise."

"Okay, but call me...for anything."

"I call you for everything," he said with a wink.

She smiled. She stood up and gave him a quick kiss before heading out of the room. She felt a bit guilty about leaving early, but there really was nothing more she could do sitting there and waiting. It was unlikely either Liam or

Rebecca would even realize that anyone was in the room until morning.

She was glad that the mystery of Liam and Rebecca's assailant was solved. It hadn't turned out to be much of a mystery, since Rebecca had been fairly certain she knew who the attacker was. She'd been right. Case closed. Justice would prevail.

If only there was justice for Rose, she thought.

It was silly, really. She just couldn't shake the feeling that something bad had happened to Rose. She hadn't given Mr. Cartwright the box of Rose's things to mail yet. Partly that was because she couldn't shake the feeling that once the box was gone any hope of learning what had happened to Rose would be gone as well.

Which was ridiculous. That's what she kept telling herself.

A new thought occurred to her. Maybe she could find the HR person at work in the morning, tell them she had to send on Rose's things, and ask for the contact information. Then she could reach out to Rose and reassure herself that the other woman was okay. And, if she happened to give the contact info to Beau...well, she was a temp. What was the worst they could do, fire her?

Unless she left abruptly to get away from someone, like Beau maybe, the thought popped up unwanted. She didn't want to think of Beau as a scary, stalker type, but given the recent events with Rebecca, how could she not consider the possibility?

She was still thinking about it when she got home. No matter what she did to try and clear her mind Rose kept coming back to the forefront, like some kind of ghost haunting her.

Cindy stared in the bathroom mirror as she got ready for bed. "Just admit it, you're not going to be able to let this go until you know the truth, one way or the other," she told her reflection.

Her phone buzzed and she grabbed it. Jeremiah had texted.

Rebecca okay. Resting in room next door. Love you.

She texted back.

Thanks. Love you. Get some sleep.

She was glad to have the information before she went to sleep. Still it didn't do anything to relieve the anxiety that was plaguing her.

There was a time when she would have thought that Rose's abandonment of her stuff was odd, but she doubted she would have leapt to foul play as a possible reason. There had been several dead bodies, diabolical plots, and non-coincidences since that time, though.

Maybe I'm just seeing murderers everywhere because I'm getting paranoid, she thought as she climbed into bed.

It's not paranoia if they're really out there, was her next thought.

Disgusted with herself she flipped onto her side and tried to go to sleep.

~

Cindy slept fitfully and when she woke in the morning she felt even more tired if that was possible. There were no new messages on her phone so presumably everything was okay with Jeremiah, Rebecca, and Liam.

She got dressed and barely managed to drag herself out the door on time. The last thing she needed was to get lectured for being tardy. She didn't know if it was just her or if everybody was in a foul mood when the security guard at work snarled when letting her in. She thought about snarling back, but decided that might not be a good thing.

She made it up to her desk, noting that she seemed to have beaten Leo, Mr. Cartwright, and pretty much everyone else on the floor. She scowled just thinking about Mr. Cartwright.

Since discovering that he was the man in the Santa suit from the picture she'd been rethinking her whole theory about Rose and Santa. Yes, Rose looked like a woman in love in that picture. And yes, Rose had put it in her pretty frame. The picture was even on her Facebook page, although it's placement stressed Rose more than Rose and Santa. For some reason, though, here at work she had put it behind the picture of her and her grandmother. If she didn't want the picture anymore she could have just thrown it away or crammed it into a drawer. The fact that it was still in the frame, though, seemed significant.

Like Rose wasn't ready to let the picture and its importance to her go.

Or like she was hiding it.

Cindy dug the piece of paper with the computer password out of the drawer since she hadn't memorized it yet.

2KC1222!

Leo had told her they changed passwords every so often for security. Until the next time to change she really should memorize this one.

2KC... 2 Kenneth Cartwrights would be 222 much! she thought.

No, that didn't take into account the 1 in front of the

222.

2 Kenneth Cartwright who played Santa on December 22 bam!

She froze. What date had the Christmas party been on? Had it been on the 22nd?

She'd been assuming that the password was randomly generated, but what if it wasn't? What if the password held some significance to Rose?

Leo sat down suddenly at his desk, startling her. She'd been so focused she hadn't heard him coming. She turned and looked at him.

"When was the last Christmas party?" she blurted out.

"What?" he asked.

"The date, do you remember? It's for...something," she finished lamely.

"Well, I left to visit family on the 23rd and it was the night before. So, it must have been the 22nd," he said.

"Thank you!"

She stared down at the piece of paper. 1222 could be a reference to the date of the party.

You're crazy, you're totally stretching, she told herself.

She turned back to Leo. "Um, Leo, are the computer passwords generated randomly for us when it's time to change them?" she asked.

"No, you'll be prompted to choose a new password. When that happens you might want to write it down because after a while they all kind of mesh together in your head and it can be a real problem."

"Thank you," she said, feeling her excitement level rising. She looked again at the password. Rose had chosen this. Most people didn't choose random letters and numbers unless they were real security nuts. This had to have meaning to her.

There were other things KC could be besides Kenneth Cartwright. A sudden memory stirred. The first time she'd logged into the computer there had been an auto-recovered document that looked personal. She had saved it and the file name had been KC.

She turned to her keyboard and quickly logged into the computer. She looked in the document folder, searching for the file, but couldn't find anything titled KC. She next did a search of the whole computer. Finally, it pulled up a document with that title.

She held her breath as she began to skim the document. It was a love letter, of sorts, although there was something off about it, not a break-up note per se, but more like Rose trying to prove to the recipient that they belonged together. It was addressed only to KC. She kept reading, hoping to find a clue that would help her solve this whole mystery. Then, suddenly, her heart leapt into her throat. It was there, in black and white, the motive.

Before she could stop herself Cindy blurted out, "He killed her."

DEBBIE VIGUIÉ

21

"What did you say?" Leo asked, startled.

"Um, sorry, nothing. Just this mystery...this story... I've been trying to...um...I've been reading," Cindy said, struggling to recover.

"Okay," Leo said, sounding less than convinced.

Cindy carefully reread the letter. In it Rose wrote very vividly about how she had succumbed to her love for the letter's recipient. She entreated him to ignore all the others who wanted his affection. Most importantly, though, she revealed that she was pregnant with his child. She ended the letter with the hope that they could be a family.

Cindy printed out two copies of the letter. The first she folded and put in her purse just in case something happened to the computer file. Then she closed the document.

She sat there for a moment, thinking. So far all she had was circumstantial evidence, and not a lot of it at that. She needed something more, proof of foul play, at the very least. She grabbed her cell and headed for the women's room.

Once there she made sure that she was alone and then called Mark.

"Cindy, is everything okay?" he asked once he picked up.

"I think a woman at my work was murdered a few days

205

ago. Have there been any dead bodies that have turned up since Friday afternoon?"

"Wait, what?" he asked. "Slow down and tell me what's happening."

"I don't have a lot of time. I'm hiding out in the bathroom so I can call you."

"Are you in trouble? I can be there in ten minutes."

"No, just can you check for me, please?"

"Okay, does this woman have a name?"

"Rose Meyer. She was in her twenties, dark hair. She was pregnant although I don't think she was showing yet."

"Okay, I'll see what I can find out."

"Text me."

"Will do."

Cindy hung up and hurried back to her desk, heart pounding. She should have thought to ask Mark sooner. She knew from the trial that she'd been a juror on that if you didn't have a body you needed to have a lot of solid evidence to even begin to try someone for murder.

She hoped she was wrong. She hoped that Mark would be able to somehow find Rose alive and well and just royally pissed off at her old employer.

Her stomach was twisting in knots as she waited for confirmation one way or the other. Her mind was just churning away, wondering how she could get a confession out of the man.

Mr. Cartwright was getting married on Saturday to the boss's daughter. He couldn't afford to have Rose and her child interfere with that.

He should have thought about that back in December, Cindy thought in disgust.

Mr. Cartwright still hadn't come in yet even though

he'd lectured her about being ready early in the morning. Every time she heard someone walking or Leo moved in his chair she nearly jumped out of her skin.

She tried to focus on organizing the documents on the computer which seemed to be in as much disarray as the papers in her desk had been. She kept glancing nervously at the clock.

Finally her phone chimed. She grabbed for it, nearly dropping it in her haste. It was a text from Mark.

No female bodies.

She slumped in her chair. She was wrong. She had been so sure that something had happened to Rose.

Suddenly there was a chime as another message popped up.

A Missing Persons Report was filed by roommate for Rose Meyer on Tuesday.

"I knew it!" she whispered, clutching her phone so tightly her hand started to shake.

Call me.

Cindy stood up and hurried to the restroom. There was someone already in there and Cindy spent what seemed forever staring in the mirror and pretending to fuss with her hair while she waited for the other woman to leave. As soon as she had she dialed Mark.

"Finally!" he exploded. "What have you gotten yourself into?"

She hastily filled him in.

"I agree that's suspicious, but without a body or a confession, we don't have a ton we can go on at this point," he said.

"So, what, we wait for the body to show up?"

"We can do some aggressive follow up on the Missing

Persons report, but without something more concrete, we're just going to have to wait."

"Mark, some poor girl is marrying this creep in two days. We have to stop him before that."

For all she knew the bride could be just as big a monster as the groom, but still, she deserved to know what she was walking into.

"Cindy, you're not thinking of doing something reckless are you?" Mark asked, voice laced with suspicion.

"When do I ever do anything reckless?" she asked.

"Flying off to Israel last summer comes to mind," he said sarcastically.

"Look, that was different."

"Why are you so upset? Why are you caring so much about this?" he asked.

Cindy paused, trying to come up with an answer, not just for him but also for herself.

"Secretary's Day is next week," she blurted out.

"Excuse me? What does that have to do with anything?" Mark asked, sounding genuinely bewildered.

"Most of the time secretaries get ignored or taken for granted despite how much they do. We are not the executives or the ones in charge. Sometimes people think that because of that we are replaceable. Interchangeable. Look at the stupid temp agency I'm working for. A secretary gets sick or fired and the company calls them and has them send a temporary one over. Like we can just step instantly into each other's shoes and know everything about the new company, the new role and responsibilities. Well, it doesn't work that way," Cindy said. She knew she was starting to rant, but she didn't care. "I earned my job at the church every single day I was there. And some new pastor comes in and thinks he knows better than me what I need, what the church needs?"

"Um, Cindy-"

"It's despicable. He wouldn't last a day in my shoes. Not one day. And then I end up here. And I'm sitting in this woman's chair, and I'm going through her things, her very personal things. And I'm just supposed to box up her life like she doesn't matter, like she never existed, and carry on like nothing happened. Well, I'm not expendable and neither was she! And if I don't push to bring her killer to justice, who will? The roommate? The guy here who was pining over her and too shy to say something? No. It always falls on the secretaries to clean up everyone else's mess, even if they don't get credit for it!"

She stopped, panting, near tears.

"Cindy, are you okay?" Mark asked softly.

"No, I'm not," she said. "I hate it here."

"Then I think you need to quit."

"I can't. Not until I've done something for poor Rose."

"You've alerted the police. You've done all you can."

She gripped the edge of the sink. "Actually, no I haven't. I think I can get that son of a...I think I can get him to confess."

"Cindy, what are you thinking?" Mark asked, panic in his voice now.

"I'm thinking Mr. Cartwright has met his match," she hissed before hanging up.

Cindy stormed out of the bathroom and headed for Mr. Cartwright's office. She didn't know what she intended to do, but she felt compelled to do something.

The door was closed but she twisted the handle and walked in. He wasn't there. Still.

Disgusted she was about to walk out when she realized that fate had smiled on her. She closed the door behind her and moved over to his desk. Maybe she could find something she could use, something that connected him to Rose.

She should have been terrified of getting caught, but she was too angry to be afraid. She sat down at his desk and began yanking out drawers.

Careful! Don't give away that you were here! a voice inside her head cautioned her.

She took a deep breath and forced herself to slow down. She went quickly but carefully, making sure she left everything as she found it. She kept going, sure that she was going to find something that would make all the difference.

Then, in the last drawer, she found what she was looking for. Underneath a bunch of books there was an envelope. It was addressed to KC. On the other side there was a red lipstick print where the sender had literally sealed it with a kiss. She grabbed a tissue off the holder on the desk and used it to carefully slide the letter inside out just a little ways without actually touching it.

She recognized Rose's handwriting. She replaced the letter then carefully put the envelope back where she'd found it. She wadded up the tissue and was about to throw it in the trash when she realized the trash was empty and he might notice the tissue and be suspicious that someone had been in his office. She shoved it in her pocket instead then rose on legs that were starting to shake and raced toward the door.

She heard the elevator chime to announce its arrival just as her hand grasped the knob. She twisted and jumped out the door, nearly slamming it behind her. A moment later she could see Mr. Cartwright step off the elevator and head her way. He glared when he saw her.

"What do you want?"

She could see the clock on the wall behind him.

"I was just coming to tell you that I was going to lunch unless you needed me right now."

He narrowed his eyes. "Fine. But be ready to work when you get back."

"Yes, sir," she said, struggling to put a smile on her face. "I'll see you in an hour."

She walked toward her desk. She could hear him muttering something under his breath but she couldn't quite make it out. She grabbed her purse and headed for the elevator. The clock was ticking, and she had lipstick to buy.

~

Mark was worried about Cindy. It wasn't like her to go so crazy. He was just hoping she wasn't about to do something rash. He was about to call Jeremiah and give him a heads up when his phone rang. It was Taylor.

"Hello?"

"Detective! I'm so glad I caught you. I finally found a motel on sixth street that I think the suspect is staying at."

"What?" Mark asked, struggling to catch up.

"Mason Dunwoody."

"Oh!" Mark said, guilt flooding him as he realized that since Taylor was working from home the man hadn't realized that Mason had been found. Mark had never called him off the search. He was just about to apologize when

Taylor continued, his tone very excited.

"There's no Mason Dunwoody staying anywhere in the area. However, I found this motel where a Mason Grant is staying. I checked and Grant is Mason's middle name. So, I faxed a picture to the guy at the front desk who checked him in and he confirmed that it was the same guy!"

Mark took a deep breath. "Great work, Taylor! I can't thank you enough. I'm heading there right now."

"Thanks, detective," Taylor said, pride evident in his voice. "It took like twenty hours but I found him."

"You sure did," Mark said. "Now, take the next two weeks off like I told you to do."

"Will do. And detective?"

"Yes?"

"Thanks for believing in me."

"You're welcome," Mark said before hanging up.

Now he just had to make sure that Taylor didn't find out that his identification of Mason's hotel room happened after the standoff at Rebecca's shop. He probably should have told him the truth, but the other man had been so excited he was hoping that the win would help convince him to stay on the force.

"I hope I didn't do the wrong thing," he muttered out loud.

~

Cindy returned to work an hour later with all the pieces of her plan worked out in her mind. She'd done everything she needed to do before returning to her desk. Once there she took the copy of the letter she'd printed, put it in a fresh envelope, and addressed it to KC. Then she applied the lipstick she'd bought at the pharmacy and carefully kissed the envelope, trying to mimic the position of the lip imprint on the envelope in Mr. Cartwright's desk. That done she cut through the tape sealing the box and put the envelope into the box, placing it near the top.

Finished, she grabbed a pen and a notepad and headed toward his office with a fake smile plastered in place. Once there she knocked on the door and heard him tell her to come in. She did, leaving the door slightly ajar again.

He was on the phone and he waved her to a seat. A moment later he hung up.

"I've got a list of things I need you to do next week while I'm gone," he said.

"I heard you were getting married this weekend, congratulations," she said.

"Thanks," he said absently.

Not the enthusiastic response she would have expected from a man about to get married.

"So, you'll be away next week on your honeymoon."

"Yup. I won't be in tomorrow either. Rehearsals and all that nonsense."

"Understood."

"Okay, ready, here's what I need you to follow up on while I'm gone."

She began to take notes. Most of it was very mundane. Forward certain types of mail to certain people, trash others. Send out a follow-up memo about the time clock that had been broken. He was having all his calls forwarded to her. He specified which types of calls to direct to other people.

She had the hardest time forcing herself to write as he droned on. Mostly because she knew that the company was going to have to get someone to take over his position permanently. And because she was equally certain that she wasn't going to be there come the morning.

Still, she played her role and kept dutifully writing everything down. With every pen stroke she reminded herself to be patient. Finally he was finished.

"Okay. I'll check back with you before I leave tonight to make sure there aren't any last minute additions," she said.

"That will be fine," he said, dismissing her with a wave of his hand.

She walked out, carrying her head high.

Just a few more hours, she reminded herself.

As soon as she sat down at her desk she found it impossible to focus. She willed the clock to speed ahead to the end of her work day so that they could get this all over with. She forced herself to continue going through the computer, cleaning up files. She kept an eye out for any others that looked like they might be personal, but didn't find any.

At last it was almost time to go. She readied her desk and grabbed her purse. She purposefully left her sweater draped on the back of the chair. She stood up and then hesitated for just a moment. It was the moment of truth. Once she put her plan into motion there was no stopping. Leo was busy turning off his computer, getting ready to bolt. She envied him.

"Goodnight," she told him, wishing she could also say goodbye. That would raise suspicion, though.

"Night," he said as he headed to the elevator.

Cindy walked to Mr. Cartwright's office and knocked on the door.

"Come in!"

She entered and left the door open but approached his desk. "Did you think of anything else you need me to handle next week?" she asked.

"No."

"Okay. Oh, I'm still cleaning out Rose's desk. She had a lot of personal items mixed in with her work papers and I'm still finding some. Since you'll be gone, once I'm done packing the box up I'll get the forwarding address from HR," she said.

He looked up and before he could protest she leaned forward and lowered her voice, "Between you and me it looks like she was carrying on an office romance. There's some interesting things I've found and a letter that's sealed with a kiss."

He looked stricken.

Cindy straightened up. "Congratulations again on your wedding. I'll see you when you get back."

She turned and walked out the door before he could say anything, closing it behind her. She went straight to the elevator and called it. The doors opened and she got in. Just as they began to close she heard Mr. Cartwright's door open.

Cindy went down one floor. There she exited and waited for a moment before making her way into the stairwell. The door on her floor was positioned in such a way that she could look out and get the lay of the land before making her way out and giving herself away.

She was able to poke her head out very slightly. Mr. Cartwright's door was open. She closed the stairwell door and stood, perched on the landing, waiting. He was the last person on the floor. Unless she missed her guess he'd go straight for the box trying to find the letter.

She waited another five minutes and then slowly opened the door and poked her head out again. Mr. Cartwright's door was closed. She stepped out and closed the door gently behind her. She took a few quick steps so that she could see the rest of the floor. There was no sign of movement by her desk.

She made her way swiftly there and then opened the box. She could tell instantly that items had been moved and the letter was gone. She closed her eyes, a thrill of excitement surging through her followed quickly by a burst of nerves. She straightened and grabbed her sweater.

It's show time.

She walked over to Mr. Cartwright's door and knocked loudly. She heard a muffled exclamation from inside and she pushed the door open. He was stuffing the envelope into his desk drawer, his face beet red.

"I forgot my sweater," she said, hoisting it up. "Then I realized that I forgot to ask you who I have sign off on my invoices for the temp agency while you're gone," she said.

"Give me your hours for this week and I'll sign off on it."

"But it's only Thursday," she protested.

"That's right. You're fired. I'd like you to stay late and ready your desk and your notes for the girl who will replace you," he said.

Cindy raised an eyebrow. "Actually, I can't stay."

"Well, then I want-"

"And you can't stay late either," she said, cutting him off.

He looked up at her, irritation written all over his face. "What on earth do you mean?"

She put her hands on his desk and leaned forward. "What I mean is that you're going to jail. You're going straight to jail, as in do not pass "go" and do not collect two hundred dollars."

"What?" he asked, startled now.

"I know you killed Rose," she said.

He stared at her for a long moment. She thought he was about to deny it when all of a sudden he lunged up from his chair and grabbed her shirt.

22

Cindy screamed and jumped backward. Cartwright held onto her shirt and came across the desk. He backhanded her across the face and pain exploded behind her eyes.

"How dare you!" he shouted. "You think you can take me down? You think others haven't tried before you?"

"Help!" Cindy screamed at the top of her lungs.

"There's no one here. Everyone who works here hates their jobs. They all run away as fast as they can when it hits five. You are alone, my dear. Now tell me, how did you figure it out!"

He grabbed her and shook her hard. Cindy kneed him and he let go of her. She turned and ran from the office, heading for the stairs. She had almost reached them when the door to the stairwell flew open and Beau stepped out in front of her.

"Help me!" she screamed.

"Stop her, she just robbed me!" Cartwright shouted.

"He killed Rose."

Beau looked past her. "Is this true?" he asked.

A shot rang out and Beau fell, blood spreading across his chest.

"Lovesick idiot, always poking your nose into other people's business," Mr. Cartwright growled.

She heard the sound of the gun cocking and she turned, hands raised to her shoulders.

He leveled the gun at her. "Tell me how you knew," he said, face contorting in hatred.

She moved slowly, forcing him to turn to keep the gun trained on her. "Her stuff."

"What do you mean? The letter?"

"The letter. All of it. A woman with so little in life doesn't easily abandon what she does have. There was no reason she didn't take those things with her. The necklace, the picture frame, the trinkets, the clothes, the personal documents. She didn't leave those willingly and if you had fired her security would have watched her clean out her desk."

He snarled. "But how did you connect her to me?"

Cindy kept moving, kept forcing him to turn until his back was to the stairs. "Her password for her computer. It was your initials and the date of the Christmas party."

He just stared at her. "So?"

"Then there was the picture from the Christmas party. Her sitting on your lap while you were dressed as Santa. She was clearly a woman in love."

"Stupid girl. All I had to do was say three nice words to her and she practically threw herself at me."

"She was hurt, grieving the death of her grandmother, you took advantage of her."

"And she was stupid enough to get pregnant, to think I'd leave my fiancée for her."

"You should have done it. Then you'd have a wife and a child and wouldn't be about to go to jail for murder with neither."

He sneered. "I'm not going to jail. I got rid of one body, I can do it again."

"And how are you going to explain Beau's

disappearance and mine?"

"Everyone knows Beau was pining after Rose. I'll just spread the rumor that they ran off together. Everyone will believe that."

"And me?"

"You're just the temp. No one will even know that you were here."

"Boy, are you an idiot," a familiar voice called out.

Cartwright turned, a shot rang out, and he fell to the ground clutching his hand. Cindy looked behind him to Mark who was standing there, his gun still trained on him.

"You okay, Cindy?" Mark asked.

"You're late," she said, heaving a sigh of relief.

"Yeah, well that security guard at the front was a real piece of work. I finally told him if he didn't let me through I was going to arrest him as an accessory to murder."

"At least you made it."

On her lunch break she'd called Mark again and arranged for him to arrive immediately after she accused Cartwright. She had panicked when he wasn't showing. Thankfully he had made it in time.

"Who's the guy by the stairs?"

"Beau. He works here. Is he...?"

"Still breathing from what I saw. Ambulance is on the way." Mark addressed Cartwright. "Hey, scumbag, you have the right to remain silent."

As Mark read him his rights Cindy collapsed into a chair and thanked God that her plan had worked.

A couple of minutes later paramedics and more officers were on scene. As two officers started to lead Cartwright away Cindy called out to him, "Oh, don't worry. I'll have your replacement box up your things and send them...somewhere."

~

The next morning Cindy visited everyone in the hospital. The night before she hadn't had a chance. Jeremiah was furious that Cindy hadn't let him in on her work stunt. Mark was coming in for a bit of that rage as well. After a late dinner and promises from both of them not to do something that stupid again he finally calmed down.

Beau had been shot in the shoulder, but was going to be okay. The far greater blow he had been dealt was hearing the truth about what had become of Rose. Mark was working overtime trying to get Cartwright to reveal where exactly he'd buried her body. Beau was broken up about that as well. Cindy felt for him. Closure was sometimes not as easy to get as one would hope for.

After seeing him she visited Rebecca who was awake and sorrowful for everything that had happened. Cindy tried to tell her that she needed to stop blaming herself for what had happened. She wasn't sure the other woman was listening.

"Look, you're going to be okay, the doctors are saying that Liam is going to be okay, we're all okay," she said, struggling to bring comfort but not feeling like she was being very successful at it.

"It's my fault. I should never have dated Mason, then none of this would have happened," Rebecca lamented.

"I don't understand that actually," Cindy said, tired of giving her platitudes.

"What?" Rebecca asked.

"How did you ever end up with a guy like that?"

"I've asked myself that a thousand times."

"And?"

"I could say that in the beginning he was different. He was charming, attentive, and it was nice. I could say that I was naïve, that I missed the warning signs or only saw what I wanted to see."

"But?" Cindy prompted.

Rebecca sighed. "While I'm sure all those things played a role, there is one inescapable truth. Sometimes we pick the wrong person to provide us comfort."

Cindy blinked. That was what had happened to Rose. Cartwright had said that he said kind things to her and she fell into his arms. While she was sure he'd been a little bit more purposeful in his pursuit than that, it was still true. She had looked for comfort in the wrong place. If only Beau had spoken up about how he felt maybe things would have ended differently. Then again, maybe they wouldn't have.

"You never know for sure how changing the past would affect the present," she said.

"What do you mean?"

"If you had never gone out with Mason, maybe the whole chain of events that ended with you living here, opening the tea shop, and meeting Liam would have been disrupted."

Rebecca blinked. "I hadn't thought about that. It was because of him that I quit instead of signing up for another tour."

"See, if it weren't for Mason, you and Liam might never have met."

"A silver lining?" Rebecca asked, a faint smile finally

touching her lips.

"I'd say a big one," Cindy grinned.

Rebecca's smile broadened.

"Okay, I'm going to go say hello to Liam," Cindy said.

"Tell him I love him."

"Okay," Cindy said.

She walked into Liam's hospital room and she found him scribbling furiously in a notebook. On the tray that normally would hold food he had spread out the papers from Mark.

"Rebecca says to tell you she loves you," Cindy said.

"She does?" he asked, looking up with a smile.

"Yup, she really does. Any luck on those?"

"A little. The code is very complex. I've only just gotten through the one letter that Paul sent to his ex-wife. I was about to call Mark. It talks about a safe deposit box."

"Where?"

"I haven't decoded that far yet. This is a doozy."

"So, where did you learn to break codes?"

"My grandpa," he said absently.

"You know, I have a feeling there's a story there."

"More than one," Liam said before turning his eyes back to the papers.

Well, so much for getting that story, she though wryly.

"You know, why is it when you knew Rebecca had a stalker that you were so adamant that no one talk to the cops about it?" Cindy asked.

That got Liam's attention. He looked up and frowned. "I said that?"

"Yes. 'No cops.' More than once, apparently."

"I guess it's because..." Liam drifted off then scowled. "Medication. Must have made me out of mind."

That's definitely not what he was about to say, Cindy thought. She decided not to push.

"Well, I'm glad you're doing better now. I'm going to go take care of a few things," she said.

"Back to work?"

"No. I called the agency and let them know what happened at my last assignment. I told them I'd be taking next week off."

~

Cindy spent a couple of days mostly sleeping with occasional hospital visits. Then she spent some time with Traci and the kids which helped lift her spirits. The days flew by and Wednesday finally arrived. It was Secretary's Day and she couldn't help but think again about poor Rose.

She was just about to head out to go to the store when the doorbell rang. Surprised, Cindy went to the front door to see who it was. Through the peephole she saw Geanie.

She opened the door. "What on earth are you doing here?" she asked.

"I've come to take you out to lunch."

"Shouldn't someone from the church be taking you out to lunch? After all, it is Secretary's Day."

"First, they call it Administrative Professionals Day now. Second, I'm the graphic designer so I don't count. Third, I'd rather spend my lunch today with you."

"Okay," Cindy said, unable to hold back a smile. "Let me grab my purse."

A minute later they were in Geanie's car zipping down the road. At her insistence Cindy filled her in on everything that had happened in the last couple of days. She had just finished when they pulled into the parking lot of Kit's, a steakhouse in town.

"Wow, fancy," Cindy said as she got out of the car. "I think I've only eaten here once before."

"Well, order whatever you want, because it's my treat," Geanie said brightly.

They walked inside and it was more crowded than she would have expected for a Wednesday afternoon. Looking around, though, she realized that a lot of the diners were bosses and their secretaries. The restaurant was high-end but it had a fun, Old West theme to it. Rustic was a good word to describe how it felt. She smiled just being there.

"Reservation for Coulter," Geanie said when they reached the podium.

"Right this way," the hostess said, a stack of menus in her hand. They followed her to the back of the restaurant and into a private room where there was a single table set for fifteen.

"I might have invited a few more people," Geanie said with a grin as she sat down.

"Who?" Cindy asked as she sat next to her and the waitress began putting menus down at each place.

"Here they are now," Geanie said.

Cindy turned and was shocked to see members of the church staff filing in. They were followed by several of the ministry leaders. They all took their seats. Cindy looked from face to face in bewilderment. They were all there except for Ben, the pastor.

"What is going on?" Cindy asked Geanie who just smiled and shook her head.

Cindy turned to Sylvia, the business manager. "Why are you all here?" she asked her.

Sylvia smiled and cleared her throat. The entire group fell quiet. "That's quite simple, actually. We're celebrating Administrative Professional's Day."

Geanie actually giggled.

"I don't understand," Cindy said.

Dave, the youth pastor, spoke up. "We're here to right a wrong."

"We're here to solve a problem," Jesse, the head of the women's ministry, added.

"Turns out nobody at the church can agree on anything," Drake, the head of the men's ministry, said.

"Except that things are a total and complete mess," added Carl, the janitor.

"And there is only one solution," said Harold, who was a Shepherd and the head usher.

"We're here to ask you to come back," Danielle, the head of the children's ministry, said.

"*Beg* you to come back," Associate Pastor Jake corrected her.

Cindy looked from face to face. Those who hadn't spoken were nodding vigorously in agreement with those who had. "That's...how is that possible?" she asked, stunned nearly to speechlessness.

"We've made it clear to the pastor that if anyone's leaving First Shepherd, it's him," Gus said. "After all, we've lost pastors before. No big deal. We can't afford to lose a secretary, though," he said with a wink.

Cindy couldn't help but smile. Gus was referencing the fact that the previous pastor, Roy, had quit because she had challenged him and Gus to stop feuding with each other.

"And he was okay with that?" she asked, feeling a warm glow starting to spread through her.

"Let's just say that I let him take a look at the books, a good look at the books," Sylvia said. "He got real clear real quick on the fact that the church couldn't afford to piss off its biggest donor over something like this."

"Biggest donor?" Cindy looked at Geanie.

Geanie grinned. "That would be Joseph. Well, now, Joseph and me," she said blushing.

"But we had all discussed before that," Loretta, the organist, hastened to add. "First Shepherd isn't the same without you. We're not happy, the congregation's not happy."

"And the room assignments and master calendar are totally messed up," Jordan, head of the single's ministry, piped up.

"Oh heavens," Cindy said, rolling her eyes as she imagined just how bad they could be.

"You have no idea, they had us trying to lead choir practice in the second grade room last week," Sabrina said.

Cindy had an image of the entire choir sitting on the teeny, tiny plastic chairs in that room and almost lost it.

"So, Cindy, will you make us the happiest church in the world and come back to us?" Sylvia asked.

Tears welled up in her eyes. "Yes," Cindy said.

As if on cue waiters appeared bearing plates filled with prime rib and mashed potatoes. They set them down on the table and Geanie beamed at her. "I ordered yours extra rare."

"Thank you," Cindy said. "For everything."

"What are best friends for?"

Cindy hugged her tight and only the aroma of the prime rib was able to entice her to let go.

Associate Pastor Jake prayed for the food and then they

all started to eat as though they were famished. After a couple of minutes Geanie picked up her glass of water off the table.

"To the return of the good life at First Shepherd," she toasted.

Cheers burst forth and everyone happily clinked glasses.

"Oh, and tell her the best part, Sylvia," Geanie said after drinking some water.

Sylvia beamed at Cindy. "Your position comes with a raise," she told her.

"Wow."

"Don't worry," Dave said with a grin. "You're worth your weight in gold."

"In that case it better be a very big raise," Cindy said.

Everyone laughed and cheered. She could feel her grin getting bigger as everyone laughed.

~

Lunch ended up lasting until the end of the workday. At that point everyone left and Geanie took her back home.

"It looks like Jeremiah is here," Geanie commented as they pulled up outside the house.

Cindy was surprised. "We didn't have plans tonight."

"Maybe he decided to drop by and surprise you," Geanie said.

"Really? You wouldn't have had anything to do with that, would you?" Cindy asked.

"Nope. He did know about your lunch surprise today, though. Maybe he wanted to be here to congratulate you in person as soon as you got home."

"Could be," Cindy said as she got out of the car.

"Thank you again, for everything."

"You're welcome, truly. I was going crazy there without you, to be honest."

Cindy gave Geanie a hug, gratitude nearly overwhelming her.

"So, I'll see you at work tomorrow?" Geanie asked.

"Nope. Monday. I'm taking a few days off."

"Sounds like a good idea. Have fun."

Cindy got out of the car and walked up to the house. As she opened the door her nostrils were immediately assaulted by the smell of fresh paint. She stepped inside and Jeremiah appeared from the kitchen with a grin on his face.

"Well?" he asked.

"I'm a church secretary," she said.

He hugged her and picked her up. "Congratulations," he said.

"Thanks," she said as he put her down.

"I'm going to feel a lot better having you work next door again."

"Me, too," she admitted. "So, what's going on?"

"Well, I'm here to take you to a movie and dinner to celebrate. First, though, I have a surprise for you," he said.

He grabbed her hand and pulled her into the living room. All of the old landscape paintings had been taken down. In their place were new pieces. The most striking was on the far wall. It was a picture of Jerusalem at dusk with the Temple Mount clearly visible. Her throat constricted as memories came flooding back. It wasn't the danger and the fighting that she remembered. It was that first kiss with Jeremiah.

There was a portrait of Captain and Blackie sitting

together that caught her eye next. The cat was nestled between the German Shepherd's front paws and they looked so adorable together.

She stepped farther into the room so that she could get a better look at the picture above the sofa and began to shriek with laughter when she saw it. It was a picture of dogs playing poker.

Jeremiah started laughing, too. When he finally stopped he said, "We can add to them or change them as you want. I thought these were more...us."

"Thank you," she said, walking over to kiss him.

"You're welcome."

"Where's the paint smell coming from?"

Jeremiah suddenly looked a little sheepish. "Well, I hope you're not mad."

"Okay," she said, her curiosity really aroused.

He grabbed her hand and led her to Geanie's old room. There was plastic on the floor and the walls had a fresh coat of pale green paint on them.

"I figured this room could be my office. I'm going to start decorating it and furnishing it. By the time I'm done we'll be getting married."

Tears sprang to her eyes. "I love it."

~

Mark's heart was in his throat. Liam had been able to decode the letter Paul had sent his ex. In it he told her about getting his letters from his lawyer. He'd also said that the key went to a safe deposit box in Sacramento, about half an hour from the home of the attorney Paul had used. Mark had taken the day to go up there. He was standing in the bank's vault, the key in his hand, staring at the box on the table.

The banker who'd helped him had left. It was just him and whatever secret Paul was still harboring. His hand was shaking slightly as he opened the box. Suddenly a step sounded behind him. He spun around just as the banker who'd led him down their stabbed him with a knife.

"A woman was supposed to come for that," the man hissed.

Mark swung with his left hand, the man blocked, but missed the fact that Mark had grabbed his gun with his right. He hit the banker in the head, knocking him out cold. He yanked the knife from his shoulder. The wound wasn't bad, but blood was pooling on the floor.

He should call for help, get the police down there.

He was willing to attack me because I wasn't the right person.

Something was very wrong here. He had no way of knowing if he called for help who would come running and which side they'd be on.

Mark turned back to the box. He needed to find out quick what the banker was willing to kill him over.

He opened the box. The only thing in it was a piece of paper. He pulled it out, hoping it wasn't another one of Paul's coded pages. It wasn't.

Mark stared down at the piece of paper he was holding. His hand was shaking so badly he could no longer make out the words. He didn't have to, though. They were burned into his memory, etched there for all time. He closed his eyes and still could see the words there before him.

"Why didn't you tell me?" he asked as he fell to his

knees.

The paper slid out of his hand and he could hear it fluttering to the floor. The sound it made when it landed seemed louder than any gunshot he had ever heard. He opened his eyes. The paper had fallen half on top of the pool of blood. The blood was already seeping through and for one terrible moment the words lit up as though written in crimson flame. In that moment he knew the terrible truth, and nothing would ever be the same.

Paul had a son.

.

Look for

NOW YOU SEE ME

the first book in the ABRACADABRA trilogy

Coming February 2017

Look for

THE LORDS OF ATLANTIS

the next Tex Ravencroft book

Coming Spring 2017

Look for

THE SUMMER OF RICE CANDY

the next Sweet Seasons book

Coming Summer 2017

Debbie Viguié is the New York Times Bestselling author of more than four dozen novels including the *Wicked* series, the *Crusade* series and the *Wolf Springs Chronicles* series co-authored with Nancy Holder. Debbie also writes thrillers including *The Psalm 23 Mysteries,* the *Kiss* trilogy, and the *Witch Hunt* trilogy. When Debbie isn't busy writing she enjoys spending time with her husband, Scott, visiting theme parks. They live in Florida with their cat, Schrödinger.

CPSIA information can be obtained
at www.ICGtesting.com
Printed in the USA
LVOW13s1541290617

539816LV00010B/720/P